Signature

"Now us, we's what's knowed as butchers."

—Micah

Copyright 2007 *by*

Ron Sanders

ISBN: 978-0-6151-5653-8

ronsandersartofprose@yahoo.com

also by this author:

Freak

Microcosmia

Carnival

The Deep End

Legerdemainia

ronsandersatwork.com

Signature's Chapters

Chapter One

The Group

Picture a man on a brightly lit catwalk.

He'll be a black man, around sixty, dressed in ceremonial robes of blinding gold. In the background you'll see a forest of upturned faces, a frozen pyrotechnic flare, and a full moon hanging fatly in a crystalline sky.

Now pretend it's a real-time image.

See that flare get blown to shrapnel, watch the crowd rear back and roar:

"Thirteen…twelve…"

Zoom out, in your head.

Imagine a couple of screwballs, on a dock twenty feet below that catwalk, hilariously arguing physics, mob mentality, and plague stats, the way you and I would go on and on about faceball scores, chickie chambers, and a good old bare-knuckle carrier-whooping.

"…eleven…"

Grab a breath and get ready. Because there's something in the air, man. There's something about the next number that obliges you to holler in sync, as if its place in the sequence holds a magical significance for anyone who can count.

"…Ten…"

And you're in! Throw back your virtual head.

"...nine..."

There's that sweet party moon, with her winking corona of satellites—

"...eight..."

—catching and bending the sun, reflecting it—

"...seven..."

—onto a thousand lunar mirrors—

"...six..."

—perfectly spaced, servo-aligned—

"...five..."

—to spell out our holiday message.

"...four..."

And there it is: written bright-on-white—

"...three..."

—and right on time. So shout it out!

"...two..."

Let go, pal! Howl like a lunatic.

"...one!"

No, damn it, *scream* it:

"And that," said Abel, "was that." He snapped his fingers. "Less than that. An instant, the wink of an eye, and…gone! Once again the crowd's immortalized a moment that exists solely as a symbol of its own pinwheeling mortality. Why can't we dedicate a day to something that *mellows* with age, eh, Doctor?" He rammed the psychoanalyst into the crowd, and someone unseen rammed him right back. The return impact bounced Abel off the throng's opposing flank, incidentally knocking Izzy back on track. In this manner they crossed the dock like a wobbly old wheel.

Every party has its bullies. The one who came after Abel was no drunker than the rest, just uglier. He shoved Izzy so hard the doctor shot through the press of flesh and was doubled at the east rail. "You push this little freak on me again and I'll kill you. Do we understand each other, old man?" A second later he was gone, swept up in the jostling promenade.

Abel called after him, "I'll push the little freak on anyone I want!" and carefully stepped around the strolling families and hooting rowdies, muttering, "and I'm not yet fifty." A few rubbernecks at the rail were slow to part. "Air," Abel explained. "Just a little room, please. He'll be fine."

Now a flurry of rockets crisscrossed the night sky, momentarily lighting the Burghs a ghastly white-and-purple. Izzy raised his streaming eyes. Not two miles away lay the Colony, denuded on the surface, but peopled below by a race hidden for so many generations it was recognizable only in folk legends and bedtime horror stories. *"Hullo, megalopolis!"* he bawled. Every drunk within earshot cheered, urging him to complete the old salutation. Izzy inhaled until his eyes were popping. *"And burn in hell, you stupid plague Colony!"* Fists were raised, empties hurled, throats screamed raw.

Izzy rocked back around, his jaw dropping at the flash of gold. "Speak of burning. What in the who is that?"

The man on the catwalk looked like he didn't know which way to spit. Fireworks were going up all over the place, but he didn't raise his eyes. Everybody else went nuts.

"Okay. That's our guy." Abel waved his arms, showing five fingers on one hand and two on the other. Security at Gate 7 immediately began ushering patrons to adjacent gates. There were garbled protests and a few shouted threats. Abel watched impassively before turning to study the black-and-gold gargoyle. "Lost in a crowd. Sad, really. The party's just starting, and there he stands; without a friend or a clue."

"Surfeit of study," Izzy gasped. "Now you hold steady! Don't you...barrass me."

Head of Security rolled his forearms one over the other. "We're on," Abel said. "Wipe your chin." He looked up at the catwalk and a broad smile cut his face in two. "Moses! Moses Amantu!" Cupping his hands round his mouth, he called over the crowd, *"Professor!"* and lustily climbed the gangplank. Abel swung round the gatepost and approached the startled historian like an old friend, his hand extended warmly.

Amantu's head jerked back a notch for each step advanced. When the two were face to face, Abel panted happily, "My name's Abel Joshua Lee, Professor, but my pals just call me Josh. I also go by 'AJ'. We're from Titus Mack." He pointed at his partner, now inching up the gaily adorned gangplank. "That's Israel Weaver there, psychoanalyst extraordinaire and my best damned friend on the planet." As if reading Abel's lips, Izzy gave a cheerful wave-back, then jumped and laughed at an abruptly-launched Screamer behind him. Clinging to the rail, he renewed his laborious climb, bending forward and backward like a punching clown. "Ti—Titus, that is—said you'd be expecting us. He might have just mentioned us as the other two members of a little frat he founded, known colloquially around the Burghs as the 'Group.' Kind of makes us sound both standoffish and regular at the same time, don't you think? Anyways, I'm really amazed to meet you, sir." He thrust his hand forward insistently.

Amantu considered the palm as though it were a rotting lab specimen. "And to." The arm dropped. In the awkward pause a flash of magenta blew into a zillion falling stars.

"Well!" Abel's grin was killing him. "My nephew's got a big hand in particle mapping. He's cleared us with the Director on down." He snapped his fingers like castanets. "One View, all fired up and ready to go! So let's not dally. We can cruise along in comfort and with dignity. Let the masses have their hoot."

Amantu looked away from the rides, away from the merrymakers, away from all things insufferably pedestrian. "These experimental amusements. I do not approve. They are dangerous, outrageously overpriced displays. I expected a cab."

"On *this*, of all days? No, no, no, Professor. You must be our guest. And the bill's on Ti. He'd have it no other way."

The black head reared. "Titus Mack demanded we ride one of these things?"

"*Well*," Abel laughed, "of course he didn't *specify* any particular conveyance. I mean, he spends so much time cooped up in that remote old observatory of his I doubt he's ever even seen a View. Look, all I know is, I get a buzz only yesterday. Ti wants to show me a discovery he's been keeping under wraps, and he's fit to bust. Haven't seen the man in a blue moon. 'Bring Izzy,' he says, 'and do me a favor. I've put out a special invite to Professor Moses Amantu of Burghsbridge, and hang me if he didn't accept. You guys hook up with him halfway and show him along.' And so of course I was excited, and reserved us a ride. Moses Matthew Amantu! Mister Up The System himself."

"And what," Amantu asked icily, "would a waveman want with an historian?"

Abel blew out his cheeks. "It's like I told you, sir. We're just here to show you along. He's got a surprise for us. And, if I know Ti, it's sure to be a good one."

Amantu's crosshairs swerved onto Doctor Weaver, now feeling his way around the gatepost. The highly-cited psychoanalyst turned out to be a balding, portly little sot with the pout of a spoiled child. Amantu made no attempt to hide his disappointment. When all three were at arm's-length, Izzy raised his eyes and winked blearily.

"Happy You Near, 'Fessor! What say you we all. Tickle old tonsil?"

Amantu looked away. "Thank you, no. I do not imbibe."

"For Cry sake, man!" Izzy's head bobbled round to Abel. "*Never?*"

The hard eyes slid back. "*Not ever!*" Faces in the crowd turned. Nostrils were flaring; a fight was in the air.

Amantu's voice cut through the din like a buggywhip. "I

do not disdain celebration, sir. Nevertheless, I feel no urge to run cartwheeling through a vomitorium simply because my calendar needs replacing. In public, *Doctor* Weaver, it is mature behavior that separates professional men from the mob. Do you not agree?"

Izzy froze as though he'd been slapped. A half-grin raised one side of his face and passed. "What you say...what you trying say I—"

Abel squeezed right in. "Perhaps we're getting off on the wrong foot here, fellows. Please accept my apologies, Professor. I so wanted to meet you congenially, and maybe absorb your brilliant theories on cultural recall firsthand. I'm certain Titus'll be fascinated." He very gently took Amantu's elbow and guided him around the gatepost.

The professor bent a kinder ear. "Oh? Mack is familiar with my research?" They picked their way down.

"Absolutely familiar. The Group has its own theories on suppressed historical data, but this work you're pursuing—wherein the brain retains, actually *hard-wires* memory over generations—well, that's the kind of stuff that gets a man in trouble. And, speaking for the Group, it's also the kind of passionate research that makes a man admired."

"Yes." Izzy and Abel descended behind Amantu, who was parting the climbing file by presence alone. "And how is it that my work has become so public?" They spilled out onto the dock.

"You know how students talk." Abel clasped his hands behind his back, affecting a cosmopolitan stroll while the New Year raved around them. "But just a word to the wise about scholarly immunity, Professor. Please have the good sense to know when the Barrier's notoriously thin skin has been breached. I'd hate to hear you'd been 'debarked,' or shot in cold blood, for that matter. Don't look so skeptical. There are perfectly credible stories of healthy, sane men being labeled as carriers. Sensible men." He squinted at a magnesium starburst. "Intellectuals."

"Stories," Amantu mumbled. "Distorted, like everything else, by the popular imagination. Recall volunteers are specifically instructed to ignore plague-related material of an anecdotal

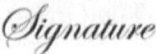

nature."

Abel nodded sourly; the professor was hooked. He steered Izzy through the crowd, studying faces all the while, and let Amantu roll on:

"*Recollection*, sir, is fundamental to our survival as a species. Memories of powerful events are therefore retained at the cellular level and passed onto descendants. Distortions *do* occur over time, but the university's equipment treats culled statements as outright lies, then uses an inversion program to reconstruct similarities into a cohesive picture. The greatest liar in the world could not construct a system of perfect liars; human beings are far too idiosyncratic. Devices do not have this problem."

"Do tell."

The professor halted. "Pardon me?"

Abel smacked his signet on the turnstile at Gate 7. The faceplate lighted, but the wheel remained locked while four softly glowing columns rose out of the deck beyond. At their apices these shafts developed horizontal limbs that extended until all four columns were linked by a misty cylindrical rail. The faceplate went dark and the wheel unlocked. Abel back-pedaled through the turnstile.

"I submit, Professor, that your conveniently receptive students are in fact carriers—and it bothers the hell out of me to have to put it so bluntly. They belong in the Colony. At least under quarantine they won't run the risk of being shot outright. Cultural recall, indeed." His fists did a spongy drum roll on the rail. "But perhaps you're doing a backhanded service. Weed out these individuals, sir, and report them immediately. Secure that university." He rolled his neck and hunched his shoulders. "Secure all universities. Anyway, let's cud some. How's about perco and a snack? Izzy, order what you like. But for Christ's sake let's talk about something else. Anything else." He flipped his hand, placing the signet and rail in direct contact. "Table for three. Destination, the Outskirts. Titus Mack's." Abel glowered over the menu. "Eight miles an hour. Transit time, forty minutes. What was I thinking? Well, we'd might as well get comfortable. Everybody move up to the rail. It says here the sensors need sixty-four square feet of clearance." They stepped back.

The map trembled with a sickly radiation. Five new columns broke the surface; one at each corner, one at dead-center. The corner posts ceased climbing at two feet, three developing foot-square seats out of their caps, the fourth broadening to form a fuzzy drink stand. The central column continued an additional foot. A horizontal plane grew out of its cap, producing a perfectly square tabletop.

Amantu tucked in his robes. "Delightful."

The View's deck commenced a gratingly slow extension from the dock, its eerily pulsing tip marking time with a tracking pulse miles away. Though the Group were soon rising gently over the Burghs, there was no real sense of being air-borne; rather, cruising on a View gave one the feeling of riding uphill in a rickety amusement park train. Still, there were brief moments of an exhilarating weightlessness, every hundred yards or so, when the deck was electromagnetically nudged by a massive ground arbor. But even that exhilaration soon gave way to a kind of rhythmic nausea.

Dozens of these bile-green arcs were rising every which way over the city, most conveying parties of drunken screaming celebrants. Rented space above Views erupted with holographic pyrotechnics, with laser-driven pixel images, with briefly reflective messages of a recklessly-publicized personal nature. And now, swimming along in that wide popping sky, the good old moon was back to her familiar unadorned self.

Abel rapped his signet on the table. "Order."

A life-sized projection appeared; half mannequin temp-late, half pretty brown-eyed waitress. The template-side scrolled through a spectrum of sample types before adopting a mirror copy. Pen poised eagerly over pad, the recovered Pj gave Abel its full attention. "Blonde," he said. "With pigtails. Blue eyes. Native blouse." These details applied immediately. The project-ion's posture and expression remained in type.

"Perco all around, please. Blue Mountain in china. You may leave the pot."

Izzy rolled back his head. "None of your blasted greasy brown beans for me, Josh! I *mean* it, man! Your embarrass us. We're aluminaries, damn it. So let's…*get* aluminated!"

"Make that a Lazy Sun," Abel drawled, "for our glowing friend. And a plate of sweet cakes. Something luminous."

The Pj made as though deleting a line.

Izzy threw an exaggerated wink at Abel, reached around cagily, and slapped the likeness on its apparent bottom. "*Okay*, 'Sweet Cakes'?" His hand, passing through, skipped across the tabletop like a stone on a pool. Izzy pitched off his seat and landed on the fat of his back. His tough little skull bounced hard on the deck.

The waitress appraised him uncertainly, then took in the table in general. A second later she broke into a mosaic of inter-locking facial samples, and was immediately replaced by the image of a towering policeman, its entire head locked up in a shiny black helmet and visor. The telepresence stared hard at Izzy, ignoring the rest of the Group. "Signate?"

Abel sat right up. "That would be me, officer. Um, Happy New Year. I'm responsible for Doctor Weaver here. He'll be fine."

The Tp only intensified its study. In a minute it was replaced by an equally-grim apparition in medical smock. A ruby beam lanced out of this image's mock ophthalmoscope. For a wild instant Izzy's sprawled body became a living anat-omy chart; every nerve, every blood vessel, every bit of carti-lage beautifully delineated. The beam dimmed and the medical Tp vanished. The cop reappeared in its place. "Signate?"

"Here."

"This individual requires monitoring. Be wary of further impairment."

"Done."

The Tp was displaced. Abel bounced his forehead re-peatedly on the table.

"Eminent," Amantu muttered.

Izzy had just found his stool when the waitress re-appeared, a misty chest in her hands. Abel touched his signet to the lid's imprimatur. The chest waxed solid and the waitress dissolved.

Pressing the lid released a thin tail of steam and the bland aroma of instant coffee. The cups were disappointing little inverse cones of disposable lined plastic, but Abel laid them out neatly, and made a show of savoring the odor as he poured. The cakes, flat dry cookies that had shattered with the release of pressure, boasted the Escalateur Company's arcing View logo in green sugar sprinkles.

Izzy gloomily unzipped his pouch and poured the vodka-rum mixture into one of the neat little plastic glasses. The accompanying pouch of freeze-dried ingredients revealed lemon-flavored seltzer powder, a packet of chipped honey, and a petrified cherry with a hollow sulfur-tipped stem. These items he poured into the liquid, then lit the floating cherry's stem with the included striker. The brandied drupe flared and sizzled, causing the bubbles of bicarbonate to glimmer and the honey to glow. He studied the sorry concoction for a few seconds before knocking it back.

"We three grown men," Amantu said through his teeth, "have just been admonished, in the space of only five minutes, by no less than two officials!"

Izzy hurled down his glass. "To hell with 'em!" The plastic tumbler didn't crack, but sprang back feebly. "To hell...to hell *alla* them!" He turned on the professor. "And to hell with—"

"Doctor Weaver!"

Izzy glared one to the other. He tore the flask from his vest's pocket.

The professor pushed his coffee aside. "Perhaps our confluence was ill-advised."

"Bladderdash!" Izzy wobbled to his feet. "The time is right!"

"Izzy!"

Corrected, Izzy cried, "The time *izzy* right!" He then appealed, at the top of his voice, to anyone within earshot: "Time to *celebrate!*" Cheers rang from proximate Views. *"See?"* Izzy screamed, losing his train of thought. "It's time! It's time! It's time, time, time! It's *time* we celebrate; it's *time!*" He snarled down at that jet-black, unflinching face. "Why izzy every jackman on planet understand but you?"

"You celebrate," Amantu seethed, "and you *celebrate*." He slapped his palms on the table. "Doctor Weaver, why an individual of your stature should celebrate, rather than cerebrate, eludes me completely."

Izzy smacked down his flask. "*Who* statue?"

Abel rose quickly. "Gentlemen. Let's remember that these festivities are not meant to commemorate time's passage in a literal sense. The mood is symbolic."

Amantu dabbed at his forehead. "The mood is imbecilic."

"*Simbasicle?* Why, you son of a...I've—I've shaken all I can!" Izzy tried to achieve a pugilistic pose while simultaneously rolling up his sleeves, rocking back and forth as he did so. "Is *human* nature celebrate!"

Tiny furnaces appeared in Amantu's eyes. "Human nature, certainly. However, this annual excuse for bacchanalia does little to aggrandize that gap between homo sapiens and the so-called 'lower animals.' Midnight on January First of the year 1347 was chronometrically destined, and, technically speaking, appeared and concluded instantaneously. The interval separating this year and last was less than a heartbeat, and I see no appreciable change in the world. Yet you *celebrate* still!"

Izzy managed to get it all out in one breath. "Then I celebrate that heartbeat, damn you, *right here and now*, and no less fervently!"

"Gentlemen! We've been all over this."

Izzy wobbled round. "No, Abel, *you* bend over for it!"

Amantu very slowly made his feet. "You damn me?" He felt his blood rising with him. "*You*...damn...*me?* Why, if you were not such a self-deluded little—" The professor was cut short by a cinching in his chest. Lava rolled down his left arm. Amantu knew the feeling well—the shortness of breath, the veil of sweat, the profound sense of morbidity. A voice addressed him from miles away.

"*Professor?*" Abel leaned across the table and peeled up an eyelid. "Doctor Weaver, you're an ass." He snatched the flask and shoved it under Amantu's nose. "Professor, I want you to drink this immediately."

Amantu raised a leaden hand. "No...I—"

"Drink it!"

The professor swallowed weakly.

"Another." Abel pushed the flask's mouth between Amantu's lips so that brandy rolled over his chin. "I've been practicing for close to thirty years, and I know the symptoms of angina when I see them. Now *swallow!*" Amantu got down another sip. Abel fell back on his stool. "Give him some air." He placed two fingers on the carotid. "Did you bring any nitro? Like an idiot, I came unprepared for the least predicament." When Amantu didn't answer he rapped his signet on the table. "I'm summoning an ambulance."

"No," Amantu gasped. "Not pernicious. I am...I am fine."

Abel couldn't buy an emergency confirmation, couldn't shout one up, couldn't wave one down. He was dangerously close to blowing his own gasket when a canned voice began rotating above the urgently throbbing tabletop—breaking up, falling out, breaking up: *signate...party of...interruption. Party of three...please...interruption...signa...signa...party of...*

"*Now what?*"

By way of reply a hazy image appeared at his elbow; stuttering with pixels, entering and deleting contours, and finally falsifying three dimensions.

The telepresence belonged to a haggard middle-aged street peddler, dressed in rags on top of rags. Affixed to his shredded trench coat were noisemakers, light flashers, and a number of fairly sophisticated pyrotechnic devices. It took him a second to get his bearings. When he saw Amantu's flashy gold robes his eyes flashed back. "Signate?"

"Outrageous!" Abel barked. "How'd you get in here?"

"Only a moment!" the Tp begged. "I have all you need, friends, to make your New Year's fete complete. Things to razzle. Things to dazzle. Things to make your party the envy of all. Or...to *really* rise above the crowd—" He threw open his coat, exposing enough fetish toys to stagger a leash of perverts.

"I repeat! *How* did you get in here!"

The man dipped a gnarly hand into an inner pocket. On his palm was an oddly glowing oval box.

"Well I'll—" Izzy marveled. "A pocket scrambler! The man's got...pocket scrambler." His head tipped back up. "Have you know, good man, that's an...ill eagle."

The peddler eyed him keenly. "And *you*, sir, will be

13

elated by the range of aqua vitae I have to offer. Cut rate, *yes!* Cut quality, *never!*" He displayed tiers of frayed body belts, each containing rows of hand-sewn pockets holding stoppered miniature carafes. The Tp swiveled the goods seductively, watching Izzy's eyes roll side to side.

Abel leaned in. "Out of the question! It's my party, and I'll make Group decisions in this matter. There'll be no contraband on my signet."

"But I've—"

"No negotiating! Beat it."

The peddler flicked his tongue and hissed like a snake. He raised his arms melodramatically, incidentally revealing a hazy row of vials clipped to a threadbare belt.

"You," Abel said quietly. "That's Swirl, isn't it?"

The image hissed again. "It's *mine* is what it is, pigeon!" Catching himself, he swept a vial filled with heaving blue smoke under Abel's nose. "Only the best, good sir! Absolutely pure, absolutely clean."

"Absolutely dilute, I'll wager. Leave it. How do I get around a trace?"

The Tp extended a banged-up signet, the only substantial aspect of his attendance. "Not a problem! Straight into my account."

Abel looked into Amantu's glassy eyes before grudgingly clicking signets. He brought his head up close and said with exaggerated clarity, "Professor Amantu, I'm aware your personal ethic prevents your indulging in certain substances. But I'm addressing your health right now. It's a medical fact that Swirl is an extremely effective vasodilator. It will quickly relieve even your most distressful symptoms. In limited use it is not only safe, it is highly beneficial. Like most medications, however, it has received a bad name through abuse. I urge you to partake of it medicinally, and with the utmost haste. It will do you a world of good."

Amantu peered through the blear. The men appeared to loom as they looked on, the whites of their eyes glowing a green jaundice from the particle map underfoot. Blue and violet skyrockets branched out behind them, erupting into fiery multicolored blossoms. The Tp sputtered and crackled. "But my mind," Amantu managed. "Will it not affect me adversely?"

"The effects are most agreeable. Consume it now and be done with it—I assure you a completely safe experience, along with a pain-free night thereafter. Understand that, in any case, I will be close by."

Amantu looked uncertainly at the eerily-lit faces. "If it produces relief...perhaps it will improve my company." He regarded the newly-corporeal vial guiltily. "Pardon me."

"Of course." Abel uncapped the little bottle and slid it over. At the disturbance its smoky contents began wafting from the mouth in a corkscrew motion. The professor drew it to his lips and hesitated. "Sip it," Abel advised, "just as you would a beverage. Only inhale as you do so." The men watched curiously as Amantu closed his eyes and tilted the vial back. The blue smoke rushed out and into his lungs. He reopened his eyes.

"Pleasant," he reported. "Refreshingly cool, with a metallic palate."

"No ill effects?"

"None as yet." He thought about it. "As a matter of fact, I am aware of an escalation in pulmonary responsiveness, and of spirit in general." He closed his left eye. The staring men became a fish-eye portrait on the lens of his right eyeball. The portrait swung smoothly to his left, sewing shut the open eyelids as it rolled. For a while all was darkness. Then, in the exact center of his skull, a vertical slice of light began widening like the crack between a jamb and opening door, rounding out as it progressed. In the midst of this light an upright black line distended correspondingly, but, rather than continuing to fill out uniformly, grew constricted in its center, so that the dark area became a sinuous squiggle with classic female curves. Amantu's breath quickened. The shape undulated in response. A heavy drum beat opened between his ears, jumping back and forth, back and forth, accompanied by a solo oboe playing an odd melody in a minor key. It took him a few seconds to realize that the drum was actually his pulse, and that the sound of the oboe was coming from the very heart of that wiggly shape. But then a dancing black woman, clad only in satiny gold bangles, was swaying side to side through a white-hot spotlight's beam, her full lips clamped suggestively round an ebony oboe's reeds, her bangles falling like leaves at every thrust and shimmy. Amantu gripped the table's edge and writhed on his seat, his breath catching in his throat. The woman blew a long ascending legato scale in reply, dropped the oboe, and threw out her arms. With her head tossed back and her lips spread wide, she shook and shook until the bangles fell from her belly, her thighs, her bosom, her bottom. The professor tensed and dropped his jaw and, for one crazy second there, was *this* close to letting go.

Chapter Two

Hammer

mantu opened his eyes to find the Group staring roguishly. Even the telepresence appeared amused. The professor pushed himself upright, his thoughts still steaming.

"A Nyear toast," said Izzy over his flask, "to Moses Mantu, Burghbridge favor son and now…now…newst member Group!"

Abel nodded. "Hear! Hear!"

"And here," the Tp responded.

"Well." Izzy searched his brandy. "Well…nickname. For Group ear, mind you, only. Let see now. Moses. Tough one. Not many great many men share suchlike forename. 'Mo?' Uh-uh. Doesn' ring. How bout 'Mosey?' Nah. Too…lay back. Are you guy help me nail this or not? We need something…meet. Something meet the man's bearing, meet the man's aplomb, the man's—wait, wait! 'Nail this,' I said. I tell you, I was on something! Man's a hammer, is what he is." He beamed all around. "And so '*Hammer*' shall be he!"

"Bravo!"

"And here."

Amantu tried to focus, but wasting emotions, normally reserved for lesser men, were gumming up his intellect. He'd never been given a positive nickname, never been accepted by anything warmer than a panel of starchy deans. That these two fine men, closer than brothers, should hold him as one of their own was inexpressibly moving. He blinked back the first tears since childhood. "You gentlemen will forgive me," he bubbled, "if I appear to blush."

Abel peered from behind his upright thumb. "Not from where I sit, you don't."

"Did I lie?" the Tp gloated. "Never cut quality!"

"You're still here?" Abel glared at the extended translucent paw. "Generally speaking, criminals don't go begging gratuities from their victims."

The telepresence ignored him. "So how's the old pump, big fella? You're okay now?"

"Odd. I feel lighter, both physically and spiritually."

"That'll be the ephedrine."

The peddler's eyes burned to the side. "Not on *your* account, signate."

"Go. You've made your sale."

The Tp threw open a ragged vest, revealing sewn-in pockets overflowing with miniature rockets and miscellaneous small firearms. "Perhaps a noisemaker or two. Something for the holiday."

"Go!"

"Half a minute!" Amantu begged. His vision had never been so keen. "Is that the barrel of an MRA, or do my eyes deceive me?"

The hawker raised an apparent eyebrow. "Oh? You like history stuff?" He slid the dully shining weapon from an armpit pocket. "Your eyes, generous sir, would make the sharpest sentry weep with envy. A vintage piece, a real collector's item."

Abel smacked down his palms and pushed himself to his feet. "That does it! You'll bring the Barrier, as well as the police. Beat it! That means *now!*" They stood nose to nose; Abel bristling, the Tp fizzling in and out of focus.

"But I *must* have it!" Amantu panted. "Eight pulses, retractable chamber, magnetic load. Where on earth—"

"I don't give a damn *where* he got it!" Abel looked the snarling illusion in its sputtering diaphanous eyes. "Get your felonious ass off my View!"

The peddler immediately tapped his grungy signet on the gun. The slender tube appeared to firm in his hand. He laid it on the table like a straight flush, his face sizzling with defiance. Amantu picked it up.

"I'll see you fry," Abel swore.

The transparency nodded in acknowledgement. "But—*until* that glorious day, signate, I've got to eat. And I like to eat well."

"Beautiful!" Amantu breathed.

Abel whirled. "Professor...'*Hammer.*' Leave it alone, man. Give it back and I'll dispose of this imaginary little crook headfirst. Understand something: that blue concoction he produced may cause you to make regrettable decisions. Decisions we may *all* regret. Please, Professor. Think how the Barrier will react if they learn intellectuals are in possession of a military weapon."

"Up for grabs!" the peddler called. "One of a kind! Won't last forever!"

"Well..." Amantu tapped his signet on the gun. "As of precisely now, it is exactly—*mine!*" He and the peddler clicked signets.

Abel sat hard. "Be gone, then!"

"Losers," the Tp sneered. "Crybabies with shallow pockets."

At this Izzy rose unsteadily, one pudgy fist poised. "And *stay* away, blast you! Where's my liba—you promised—where's my—" He picked Amantu's MRA off the tabletop curiously and raised it over his head.

The men jumped to their feet. Amantu leaned halfway across the table, Abel threw out his hands. The transparency stepped back.

Whoops rang on parallel Views. Someone yelled, "Kick his butt!" and another hurled a flask that bounced harmlessly off Abel's stool.

"Where's the hell my libation?" Izzy howled. A hail of containers blew onto the Group's View. He up-thumbed the trigger. "For Christ's sake, *where?*" The force of the discharge nearly broke his arm. A white pulse tore skyward, erupted as a bright silver jellyfish, and dissipated in a counterclockwise spiral of glittering platinum.

"*Moron!*" the Tp screamed, and was gone. Abel swore

up and down, pounding his fists on the table while Izzy turned in a slow circle, stunned. Amantu snatched back the weapon.

"What in Reason's name are you doing? This is not a toy!" He was hyperventilating. "Doctor Weaver, I arrived under the impression you were a man of character, not merely a character. In my eyes you have failed, and failed miserably, to live up to even the minimal requirements of a professional man."

"That tears it," said Abel.

Izzy looked from his empty hand to Amantu's glowering nightmare mask. His brows came together. "Sorry my. My sully my..." Comprehension dawned. "Sullied my reputation!" He flicked his fingers disdainfully, as though blowing off a malingering client. "*My reputation!*" He backpedaled clumsily while pumping his fists. Sensors instantly extended the railing, but it was too late. Izzy's substantial bottom came down just beyond the mapped lip, so that the furiously recalibrating shelf served only to help flip him into space. He vanished as he'd celebrated, throwing a haymaker at the sky.

Abel and Amantu breathlessly watched him bouncing off fleeting splotches of light.

"It is my fault," Amantu offered. "I should not have provoked him. His faculties are incapacitated."

Abel paced the rail, squatting and rising, intuitively employing the scientific method. The data were not promising: stretching View to View, and visible only through the disturbance of its tympanic vibrations, the bowl-shaped safety net was now rimmed by a remapped rail rising to an insurmountable twelve feet. Every sudden movement brought a siren's howl and accompanying bright beam.

"Nonsense. I'm supposed to be monitoring him." Abel's face went white. "Damn! I'll have to summon an emergency breach. Get rid of that weapon, Professor. I don't care what you do with it—toss it. No! There's probably a trace already. Hide it. Anywhere." He twisted a lip. At the tracking field's depressed hub, the gently bobbing psychoanalyst lay on his back in a web of briefly radiating light pulses. Over a hundred feet below, ground sensors released a storm of bright orange beams.

Abel swiped his signet across a length of blinking horizontal rail and said, very distinctly, "Breach." That portion of the rail dissolved. He clung to the active stubs like a novice parachutist.

Izzy, by rolling round and round and side to side, eventually made it to his hands and knees. He clawed ineffectually against the planet's pull, losing a foot for every two gained.

As Amantu took his deepest breath, Swirl seemed to flood into every capillary. "Pardon me." Decorously leading a golden hem, he swung a leg through the breach and set down his foot as though testing a pool's temperature. A spray of light met his sole. There was a sensation of resistance.

Abel called down, "Hold still, damn you!" Izzy feebly thrust out a hand and rolled. "I *said*," Abel screamed, "hold… *still!*"

A chant grew on those rides made contiguous by the net. "Hold *still!* Hold *still!* Hold *still!*"

Amantu was shaky as a foal. It required near-super-human focus to concentrate on his object, rather than on the gaping metropolis so far below. The experience was similar to walking on glass, in that the lack of a visible surface produced in the brain an unshakable sense of impending doom, but in another sense it was far worse; here there was not even the comforting feel of solidity. The field, active only where contacted, produced a fleeting, squishy support for the weight of each placed foot, instantly eliminating that support once the weight was removed. The effect was intensely unnatural. Amantu went straight down on all fours.

If not for Swirl he'd never have recovered. Amantu scurried down on his hands and knees, leaving bright vanishing prints. When he reached Izzy, the professor adroitly flipped onto his back, grabbed the doctor's wrists, and began hauling him along a yard at a time, using his own heels and posterior as points of thrust. The pair came lurching up to the breach. Abel, on his belly, grabbed collars and yanked. Once again the heroics were all Amantu's. The Hammer pulled himself onto the deck with a bicep in either fist, gave a mighty heave, and dragged Izzy aboard. He tried to assist the analyst onto a stool, but Izzy shook him off.

"There's gratitude!" Abel snarled.

Amantu was exhilarated. "No matter." He smoothed his

robes up and down. "We are safe and sound." He watched excitedly while a harsh light tore skyward like a rocket.

Abel cursed as he deleted the breach. The net shut down, the rail sank back to normal. "Don't," he grated, "break out the horns and whistles just yet."

Amantu would have been amazed to see the juvenile grin on his face. "Gentlemen! I am to be congratulated. This will be my debut with the police."

Izzy raised his head, a self-deluded, punch-drunk prize fighter. "'Grats."

The professor seated himself ceremoniously, but, unable to be still, ordered and re-ordered the cups and chest, inspected the table for drops and crumbs. "I suggest a show of nonchalance."

"My repu—"

"Izzy, if you don't shut up I will personally spoon-feed you disulfiram. You got me?"

The light, rising to eye-level, slowly swung round to expose three properly seated gentlemen mildly distracted by all the pyrotechnics and revelry. The glare intensified as it neared. The Group shielded their eyes. When the beam was alongside the View it waned to a rolling amber glow on a hovering chopper's handlebars. A scarlet, pencil-thin beam shone into each squinting face, resting longest on Izzy. The officer popped his scrambler from its holster and aimed it at the deck. A section of railing dissolved, quickly reforming as a broad jutting ledge. He stepped off, disengaged his chopper's emergency lights, and firmly pushed the machine down by its seat until the blur of its undercarriage melded seamlessly with the ledge. Seven feet of irresistible authority, he loomed over the dead-silent Group, the glossy black of his helmet and visor reflecting their ash and ebon faces. The visor swung onto Abel.

"You, signate, were warned to monitor."

Abel cleared his throat. "There's been no damage, officer. Our friend here simply lost his balance. He was quickly rescued and, as far as I am aware, nary a contusion resulted from the affair. Please notify your captain that my account will accommodate any expenses incurred by the ride's owners, and also your very professional work here."

The officer locked in place. An excruciating minute later the visor swiveled to Izzy. "Up."

Izzy raised his blood-red eyes. "Why, you—"

"Doctor Weaver! You are on my signet!"

"Up!"

"My reputation," Izzy snarled. *"My reputation!"*

The officer's arms spread like wings, his ramrod fore-fingers zeroing in on Izzy's temples. The twin flashes were so faint they might have been figments. Izzy's head snapped back, his feet kicked up, and he flipped off the stool onto his rear. When his eyes reopened he was dead sober.

"Up."

Izzy glared menacingly. Abel and Amantu made to assist, but froze at a jerk from that looming black helmet.

"Up!"

Izzy pulled himself to his feet.

The officer studied each man in turn. "Down!" Amantu winced as the Group took their seats. "An unauthorized firearm was discharged on this map." Nobody moved, but their eyes were all over the place.

"Up!" The officer removed his scanner and walked once around the table, sampling the standing men. "Down." The Group resumed their stools. "Signate."

"Yes?"

"Your account is cancelled."

Abel went absolutely limp.

A flurry of data raced across the polyvinyl visor. The black carapace cocked. "What was your destination?"

"Was?" Abel squealed. The night stopped on a dime. Those nearer View riders, picking up on the tension, watched quietly. "Officer. Am I—am I under arrest?"

"Up!" The mechanical voice was deadly. "The incidence of public drunkenness is waived. A discharged military weapon was traced to this map." Another flurry further straightened his back. The input ceased and he leaned back down. The voice went flat. "The courts are closed for the holiday. Due to the expected crush of cases, bail may be remitted against a suitable sponsor's account in lieu of arrest."

"Oh, *thank* you, officer!"

The helmet didn't budge. "On my discretion. Down."

Abel sat with his hands folded on his lap. "We are," he said as distinctly as possible, "on our way to visit a colleague, the celebrated astronomer and wave cataloguer Titus Mack. He lives outside the city proper, but he's a highly respected citizen. I'm sure he'd be cheerfully willing to overwrite this little misunderstanding."

"By proceeding, you agree that the request will be monitored here in my presence, and that a recording will be filed as a legal document."

Sweat broke from Abel's hairline. Suddenly he was weak as a transvestite in a holding tank. "Look, officer. It's really putting Ti on the spot, you know? I mean, couldn't we just like, laugh this off, make a New Year's resolution or two, and be done with it?" He looked down, toeing the paused map. "I really feel your demand is prejudicial."

The officer snapped to attention. "Up!" Abel rose agonizingly, swaying like a cobra. "Approach!" Abel took a timid step forward. The cop strode up titanically, bent at the waist, and got right in his face. "Raise. Your. *Eyes!*"

Abel's mousy reflection became a funhouse image on the visor's convexity. His breath fogged the acrylic, but the officer didn't move. Now sweat was flowing freely on Abel's forehead and cheeks. His knees and shoulders caved and recovered, caved and recovered. When he thought he'd faint, a whisper broke his lips. "Officer—"

"Down!"

Abel crumpled on the stool and buried his head in his arms.

In a minute Mack's voice could be heard, seemingly emanating from the air just above the table.

Titus Mack here. What's this all about?

Abel raised his head and looked around deliriously. "Ti? *Ti!* It's Abel. There's been some kind of a mix-up. We're on one of those View rides over the Burghs. Somebody shot off a rocket or something, and somehow or other we've been implicated. There's no way to clear it up right now, and anyway they've gone and cancelled my account. It's the holiday, so they're giving us the option of a sponsor over jail. Can you handle it, man? The officer's right here, and he's recording. As far as I know, we're not yet under arrest."

A pause. *Is everybody aboard?*

"Yes, we're all here."

Then of course I'll sponsor. Mack's voice cut out.

The cop raised his scrambler and rapidly tapped out a sequence using thumb and forefinger. The deck shimmered under his gleaming jackboots. Table and chairs melted in a reverse of their formation, and the ledge, now a tongue append-ed to the View, began porting the Group, officer, and chopper high over the metropolis. The officer ignored them completely, standing erect and motionless, facing away. The men stood tightly bunched. After a while their hands and feet were freez-ing. They sat very gradually, facing one another with legs crossed and heads almost touching.

Abel moaned into his cupped hands. "We're…going to jail. I *knew* it. We're *going* to *jail!*"

"Not so," Amantu gushed. "I shall gladly bear our bur-den, as my account is spotless. I assure you, my friends—the moment I encounter a magistrate these little follies will be laughed right off the books."

Two pairs of eyes looked up darkly.

"*Professor* Amantu," Abel grated, "what took place here tonight is on *my* signet. *Everything that has happened*, from the moment I scanned us onto this stupid flying snail, is *officially* on my tetherball of a head!"

"My fault," Izzy whimpered, whipping out the flask while the cop's back was turned. "Me! Me! All me!"

"Well, Izzy, hopefully the judge will take your contri-tion into account. Because, damn you all to hell, *we're going to jail!*"

It was a long ride over the metropolis. Re-keyed ground sensors delineated an official corridor to courthouse and sub-stations, complete with flashing lights and wailing sirens. The Group weren't the only ones thus escorted; similar green tongues were approaching the civic center from all directions. Some were already in the process of dissolving on police docks. It was pretty obvious the rides would be undergoing some serious rethinking after the holiday. Now the twin bloody comets of a lost ambulance, disoriented by the aerial displays, rocketed by overhead, causing proximate Views to dip and pause. The Group shakily regained their feet. The officer didn't turn. They were halfway across the Burghs' M Grid when the tongue halted abruptly, its tip suspended a hundred feet above a pulsing tower.

The officer straightened like a man being electrocuted. After a minute he came up to the Group and brought his shiny black visor in close.

"Up!"

The men watched encrypted data race across their reflections as he studied each face in turn, dwelling longest on Amantu. The cop stomped back to the tip and resumed his stance. Holding his rigid arms straight down, he pointed his scrambler at the Burghs and banked the tongue away from the sprawling Center, clear across the great expanse of the grids, toward the Outskirts' wide lonely plains.

The morning grew chillier as they rode, the landscape progressively less attractive. A bitter wind replaced the composite warmth of bustling humankind. Mystified by the proceedings, the men bundled themselves deeper into their robes and scarves, speaking only with their eyes. By the time the tongue's tip was testing the surface, the moon's misty white medallion was shining coldly on a boundless desert junkyard, and the proud torch of civilization was a wan and distant glow.

Chapter Three

The Outs

T he cop deposited the Group in a section of Outskirts known only to vagabonds and poisonous spiders. He stood straight as an arrow in his jackboots; a grim colossus staring into tomorrow.

"Signate?"

"Here."

The helmet didn't budge. "I am prohibited beyond this point in a non-emergency situation. Titus Mack has initialized a sounder. Are you receiving?"

Abel watched the soft pulse of his signet. "I have him."

"This party is hereby transferred into his custody, and from here on you are on your own. The Colony proper is fully seven miles away, but the intervening terrain poses dangers beyond police purview. You are duly advised to make directly for his mark, and not linger to satisfy your...scientific curiosity." The polyvinyl faceplate turned to Abel. "You retain, of course, the option of protective custody until the courts re-open after the holiday."

"And *you*, frothisir," Izzy snorted, "are drooly advised to take a flying—"

The black eggshell swung hard. Izzy's eyes dropped. After a long moment the visor moved along. Abel too looked down, his fists and jaws clenched. "Yes," the officer breathed.

When the faceplate reached Amantu the head moved in curiously. The professor, a man of genuine presence accustomed to gaping inferiors, automatically drew his robes tighter and returned the stare. The head kicked back. Again with the brief tweak-and-sizzle. Bringing his visor up way-close, the officer said with canned deadliness, "Happy New Year." His spine jacked straight, his shoulders squared, and then he was the same bakelite statue that had escorted them thus far. He aimed the scrambler between his boots and punched out a new sequence. The tongue's tip pulsed. The application reversed, lifting the cop and chopper off the ground and backward. Not until he'd been elevated some fifty feet and was a good hundred yards away did the Group relax.

"That," Amantu declared, "will be enough celebrating for me." He fluffed his robes. "Although I must admit I— cannot remember feeling so vigorous." He squinted into the stinking wind. "Exactly how far did he say?"

"He didn't." Abel raised his signet against the drear. "But I've got the feed. To hell with him. Let's get going."

Izzy licked his lips. "Do lead on, Josh." He swatted the dust from his vest and after a moment said shyly, "Praps somebody owes the Hammer—debt of gratitude."

"Yeah," Abel said wryly. "Thanks, Professor."

"Esteemed friends, the pleasure was entirely mine."

They were picking their way along, intuitively com- municating sotto voce, when three seemingly innocent heaps abruptly rose about them, cutting them off at the fore and flanks. Those heaps were actually camouflage: bent-round shields of aluminum siding covered with lengths of pipe and assorted greased-over debris, all attached with strands of grimy copper wire. The thugs stepping from behind these shields wore black hooded cloaks, homemade black gloves, and shabby black boots—each amateurishly patched article dyed with soot. White thread portrayed rude skeletons: cruciform stitching represent- ing stubby arms and spines, stitches on the gloves suggesting metacarpals and phalanges. The brigands' faces were painted ash-white, except for great black circular blotches about the eyes, a black ring at each nostril, and painted death's head teeth stretching from mouths to ear lobes. Crude staples affixed their hoods to skin at the foreheads, cheeks, and jaws. Out of those black eye-splotches the highwaymen's orbs gleamed like the eyes of rabid raccoons. The bandits linked hands to fence them in.

Their leader was a psychotic giant wholly ignorant of decent grammar and basic hygiene. His gloves and boots were dulled by a thousand fights and forays. But his eyes were sharp as lasers.

"Happy New Year, ladies. Sorry to disappoint you, but the theater is that-away."

Abel smiled only with his teeth. "Guys! Guys! Didn't mean to startle you. We were just on our way to visit an old buddy for the holiday, and got a little bit on the lost side, that's all." He winked and pantomimed a drunken leer. "You know how it is."

"Oh, you're lost, all right. Now, if you'll kindly lift your skirts we'll get this over with." The men submitted meekly as they were patted down and stripped of their valuables. The leader raised Abel's signet in his huge gloved hand.

"Well now, what have we here? Why, it's a wee pink eye! And she goes blinkety-blank, blinkety-blank, over and over. But what does she mean, and who does she summon? Tell me, girls—could this be some sort of diabolical signal? A secret message to your gentlemen callers, not meant for the likes of a lot of filthy old Outers?" He eyeballed each man in turn.

Abel's bark of laughter didn't fool anybody. "Aw, c'mon, man. It's a simple repetitive pulse. What kind of message is that?"

The laser eyes swung back. "I recognize this pretty little pearl, Senator. She ain't a message-maker. She's a message-taker. She's a locater! So now the issue becometh: just who wants to locate who?"

"Oh, take it then. Rip its guts out, smash it to bits. It's only a trinket; there's warehouses full of 'em. My nephew's got a big hand in camping toys. So...we'll just be on our way, and a Happy New Year to all!"

"Blinkety-blank," the man repeated, considering Abel narrowly. "Blinkety-blank, trampety-tramp, and way too much yakkety-yak. Just a caution, Senator: don't be talking in circles as well as walking in 'em. What's your business in the Outs, is what I wants to know. Why should you three peripatetic princesses come *here* a-courting? Suitable suitors, unless I'm severe-mistook, are scarce-proper in these parts. You ballerinas couldn't find amusement enough in your slick-hearted city?"

The big man's lieutenant fingered Amantu's silky gold robes. "Looky here, Micah! Ain't this a lovely dress for a girl's night out?" He curtsied for his friends, holding high his own filthy black hem.

"Why, Ezekiel! I do believes you're jealous." Micah smiled genially at the professor, the painted-on death's-head grin arching at the corners. "Maybe she'd be pleased to trade skirts."

Malachi chimed in, giggling at his own pun, "She's a pretty black, a pretty black, a pretty black p-polliwog. N-not *pretty*-pretty. P-p-p-pretty *black*."

"Vectors. You will keep your diseased hands to yourselves. Touch me even once and I will slap that silly white paint right off your silly pink faces."

Abel laughed even harder. "Fellas, fellas! The Hammer's been partying plenty hard tonight. He's not responsible for his actions."

Micah shouldered Abel aside, his face deadly. *"Diseased?"* He grabbed Izzy's collar and squeezed until it looked like the psychoanalyst's head would pop. "I'll show you disease!" As crowing Malachi leapt around them, the big man shoved Izzy along with measured brutality, Ezekiel prodding Amantu and Abel at the rear. The Group were smacked and kicked to a large mound of stacked aluminum scraps. Micah and Ezekiel maintained their prisoners in revolving headlocks while Malachi hauled aside a camouflaged gate over a black stairwell. The Group were beaten down rough steps, manhandled to their feet, and dragged along a brightening tunnel to a rock wall outside a torch-lit cavern. Inside, hundreds of voices called out in the strangest fashion, equally pregnant with ecstasy and pain.

"Welcome," said Micah, "to Dan'l's Gate." His eyes danced with torchlight. "You are expected." Ezekiel and Malachi peeled the Group off the wall and hauled them toward the bright mystery within. Izzy broke first. Screaming hysterically, he scrambled into the darkness with his friends on his heels.

In three enormous strides Micah was on them. The man's strength and energy were prodigious, but the cornered

Group, inspired by Amantu's unblinking exchanges, put up a frenzied resistance, and by the time Micah's henchmen had regained control the brunt of his fury was spent.

"*When*—" he snarled, puffing hard, "when the Cannonites walled in Jerrycho, what were their quarrels? Not to taste stone? *Why?* Are your lips too pure?" He hammered Izzy's head against a wall.

"No sir," Izzy croaked. "Not pure at all."

"Don't you spin me, Leftie! We knows you was sent by the Seizer."

"By the *what?*"

"By the Seizer! By Julius."

Abel's face twisted up in Ezekiel's chokehold. "For Christ's sake, man—what in the world are you *talking* about?

Micah booted him viciously. "*You*, reprobate! And don't you be naming him in vain. Did he die on the double-cross, or what? *Answer!*"

But it was Amantu who answered—with a hard left followed by a harder right. He almost had Ezekiel when Malachi went for his eyes. Suddenly both men were all over him.

Abel watched aghast as the professor hit the ground. "Oh, Mercies! What will you people do with us?"

"That depends on Mama." Micah clubbed friends and foes alike, smashing everybody into a pile. Revitalized, he stormed back to the cavern's opening and stood yelling with his black gloves poised like fat spiders on the rock. "They're here, they're here! Tell Mama they're here! Thirty pieces of silver is all they seek; ten for me, ten for thee, ten for the cock's crow. Tell Mama, tell Mama! Tell Mama they're here!"

A hundred voices blew into the antechamber like hot gas.

"*Mama!*"

Micah turned and pointed the finger of Death. "God's gonna getcha, He's gonna *getcha!*"

"Mercies!" Izzy screamed.

The Group broke their captors' grips by squirming and stamping, and for a while there it was all a riot of grappling silhouettes. Then Micah barked, "Mal! Get Danny!"

Malachi flapped to the wall. A latch was slammed aside.

There came a godawful rumble and clatter, and a second later a chain barricade crashed on the floor. The Group fanned in reverse while the backlit jackals pressed in with their gloved fingers wiggling, calling back and forth, "Whoo-oo-oo!" Micah's hand dipped under his robe. There was a bright gleam of metal.

"Snippity-snip, choppity-chop. Lop off the gonads, watch the boys drop."

"*Please*," Izzy whimpered, "you've got the wrong guys, you guys. We don't want any more trouble."

"Oh, we know *exactly* what you girls want. Coming for that thief Barberus, were you? Well, too bad. You already gots a date with Mama." Micah flicked the blade twice. His partners immediately rushed their personal targets, then abruptly whirled to jump Amantu. Before they could take him down, a silvery bolt blew away a chunk of the tunnel's ceiling.

The Group dashed into a well-used side-passage, and were quickly consumed by the dark. The closeness had a nauseating core: in a minute they were screaming and gagging as they hopped amidst putrefying cadavers. They crashed into walls, fell sprawling on rotting flesh, jumped up and ran headlong into an obscene darkness. The light of pursuing torches danced on projections like embers, accompanied by a clamor resembling angry bees, but the light and voices grew distant as the Group stumbled through a twisting maze of tributaries.

"Shook 'em!" Abel crowed.

"*Please*," heaved Izzy. "No more. End this nightmare." He took a massive breath. "Professor. Ah, the Hammer! Every bit the nick-of-time hero. Mercy, son. Where'd you hide that gun?"

"In a place of interest only to proctologists. I…I believe I have killed a man."

"There's a draft!" Abel hissed. "One of these tunnels breaches the surface!"

The proceeding Group used a kind of vocal sonar, sounding one another before each careful stride. Abel's selected passage wended painfully, in places narrowing to a crawlspace. Before long they were scraped raw. This profound darkness completely upset the senses. At last they paused, clinging and speaking in the tightest of whispers. It was difficult to tell who was doing the talking.

"They've given up. Not a trace of light behind us."

"A bleak victory. There is less illumination here by far."

"Who was that?"

"I. Amantu. We cannot go backward. We cannot go forward. We have placed ourselves in mate."

"Well, we can't freeze up here."

"I'm blind."

"Who just spoke?"

"Me. Izzy. I can't see a thing, you guys. If I poked my own finger in my eye I wouldn't know who did it."

"We are all blind. It is imperative we retain touch as our basic sense. I suggest personal handholds. We can move single-file, and so make our way—ponderously, certainly, but with a degree of security."

"Make our way? *Where*?"

"Anywhere but here. Let us proceed. We must find a sign of life or retrace our steps to the light. Then we must think."

"Same objection. Think about *what?* This is hopeless."

"Not necessarily so. We have brainpower, proven throughout time the superior force."

"Well, it's done some job so far."

"Who said that?"

"I did. It was me."

"Sirs! Who was *that*?"

"Steady there, Professor. It's me, Izzy. You needn't hold so closely; just keep a strong pace's distance. Then we won't be as prone to, you know, belly right up against each other and all that. No offense."

"None taken, Doctor. And yet…at arm's-length, please. Keep it at arm's-length."

"Aw, shucks. And just when we was getting all cozy-wozy."

"*Ghaa!* They are among us!"

"Ooh, la-la-*ladies!*"

"C-c-caughtcha!"

Out of the sudden riot came a whirling silver light, clearly disintegrating a patch of wall. The next instant all was darkness. Again with the sightless flight, again with the battered elbows and knees.

All else being equal, fear will always outrun anger. In time the Group outdistanced their pursuers, though they were no less blind than before, and just as lost. They moved on tiptoe, whispering only after small identifying tugs, and then only with lips pressed against ears. Finally they sat in a tight circle, their foreheads touching.

"I'm telling you, it's futile, Josh. I'm beat, man, beat."

"Quit whining. If they find us cringing here they'll kill us. I've never been surer of anything in my life."

"I concur. We are bereft of options. Perhaps…a peace offering."

"Peace offering! That's clinical psychosis sneaking up behind us."

"Absolutely. Besides, peace never solved anything. Let me see that weapon."

"A moment. Your hand. There. What do you intend?"

"How deep was that little hole they dragged us down?"

"Three, four yards. Perhaps more."

"Right. And the floors of these caves and passages have all been roughly level. If I'm not mistaken, our progress along these tunnels, when not absolutely horizontal, has been ever upward, albeit of the gentlest degree. What I'm trying to say is— we've never been far from the surface! Stand back." Abel rose, using Izzy's forehead for support.

"You are as deranged as they! Doctor Lee, you will kill us all!"

"Get *back!*"

There came another bright whanging comet, and a section of the tunnel's roof came down twenty feet away, completely blocking the passage.

"Outstanding! Not only have you eliminated our sole hope of egress, you have simultaneously announced our whereabouts to every madman in the house!"

Another pulse, and an even larger section collapsed on the first. The men backpedaled, coughing and exclaiming, while Abel fired again and again. The concussions and flashes were staggering, but he fired furiously until the magazine was spent.

"There! The sweet breath of night! Do you feel it?"

In response a posse of torch-waving lunatics came tearing up the tunnel. The men clambered awkwardly over the heaped rocks, losing precious advantage while squirming to avoid unhappy intimate contacts. More time was lost at the surface, as a decent exit now involved extensive apologies. But then a great company was spilling into the passage below, and upon their maniacal roar the Group lost all sense of decorum. They whirled and began a close sprint, elbow to elbow, heads down and rocking.

At least a dozen carriers poured out of the earth like hopped-up termites. They ran as a bloodthirsty unit, screaming bizarre slogans about smiters and martyrs.

"South," puffed Amantu, now holding the lead. "A structure of some kind."

In the distance squatted an isolated little observatory that, under the Outs' dirty white moon, resembled nothing so much as a porcelain tortoise. The running men turned in the manner of desperate over-the-hill athletes, and put their hearts into it. Yet only a hundred yards separated they and the mob, while the tiny observatory appeared a full quarter-mile away. Almost weeping with the effort, the Group threw back their heads and ran for their lives.

Chapter Four

Solomon

I t was a close race, with victory going once again to the self-preservation instinct. Yet for the final hundred yards, and especially over the last grueling seventy feet or so, the Group, middle-aged men all, were closer to death's door than to Titus Mack's. When they reached the porch, fingernails and teeth were literally at their backs.

Fortunately the place was ready for them. Both Izzy's and Abel's scans were pre-keyed, and the professor's had been transmitted and memorized upon his acceptance of Mack's New Year's invitation. The instant their feet hit the property line the observatory's hemispherical wall began to hum in anticipation. When they were a hair's-breadth from contact, the facing surface quickly breached and sealed, leaving their crazed pursuers to pound in frustration without. A breath of pressurized air escaped with an anticlimactic *pop*.

Mack's observatory was part of the old Eyeball line: basically, an outer wave-collecting "lens," a flexible central "iris" for digitizing those collected waves, and a smooth white Neoprene Inner Kinematic Surface—anagramatically NIKS, but known in the astronomical community in reverse-anagram as a "skin." Mack's skin was sympathetic; that is, it was able to learn and underwrite its runner by continuously filing domestic events as data, even as it automatically updated saved wave files.

The men blew in like tumbleweeds. No one should have been in worse shape than the angina-ridden professor, yet Amantu, still tiger-eyed and full of vinegar, was first to his feet, and the one man able to haul everyone upright. Abel, stanching the flow from his nose, coughed out, "It's only us, Titus! Sorry about the racket! Bit of a disagreement with your neighbors! Happy New Year!" Outside, the hammering diminished to a pattering like rain.

The skin vibrated. "And to!" called a voice from one of the building's concentric apartments. "Just give me a minute! Help yourselves!"

"Please—" Abel hacked back. "Take your time!"

Izzy called up a bar post-haste. The circular floor's zodiacal arrangement broke up, and a complex glass cabinet rose with a noiseless, orrery-like movement. Various menus showed round the skin and passed. Izzy bolted enough to anaesthetize a psychotic, then balanced back a tray heaped with spirits and glasses. Abel called up a favorite drink stand to meet him. The thing was a beaut; a diode-lit Messrs Ivory with a shatterproof, chlorophyll-painted lens top. The Group feigned nonchalance vociferously, hurriedly brushing their hair and robes in the glass as electronically-magnified flagella and protozoa appeared to inch along between their drinks and reflections. By the time Titus Mack came ambling in the atmosphere was almost cordial.

Half a year had passed since the Group last saw their founder, and over that span his well-kept appearance had changed dramatically. His graying brown locks were a mess; plus he'd adopted a perpetual five o'clock shadow. His comforttable paunch was gone; he'd become, through either nerves or undernourishment, gaunt by comparison. And apparently he was too busy to bother with fresh clothes or soap and water. His matted outer robe hung from stooped shoulders like laundry on a line, his sunken waist was delineated by a belt with a knee-length overhang. Underwear and unwashed plates were scattered about the floor's gel tiles. Only now did Amantu note the thousand palm prints on the skin's sloping face.

Abel threw out his arms. "Ti! Nothing like the bachelor life, eh? Sorry about the turbulent entry, but boy, did we have a time of it with the adjacent fauna. Did you know there's a Colony arm only a footrace away?"

"You didn't take the usual route?"

"It was that little run-in with the law. We were formally escorted, and not without a fight mind you, to a patch of infected real estate maybe a quarter mile north of here. Fraternal thanks, by the bye, for coming through."

Amantu rose deferentially. "Sir. You are in grave peril."

Mack waved him down. "Relax, Professor, relax. I know all about those morons. That bizarre behavior of theirs is the result of some doctored history I've been catalo—but, this is *exactly* why I wanted to see you guys this morning! And precisely why I'm so pleased to meet *you*, Professor Amantu." Titus Mack offered his famous hand.

Amantu, still hopped-up and giddy, seized it in both of his and held on overlong. "Titus Mack! An inexpressible honor! I stand, dilettante that I am, in the shadow of a legitimate legend."

Mack extracted his palm. "So they tell me." He scratched his chin thoughtfully, his eyes running over the professor's beautiful golden robes. "And a grand night for celebrating it is! I promise you a spectacle, sir; one no other company could appreciate so astutely. Unless, of course, that company just happened to include, oh, the distinguished mediator, AJ Lee, and the famous skullcracker, Doctor—" Mack abruptly threw his arms around the little psychoanalyst—*"Izzy!"*

"At service!" Izzy squirmed free. He blushed and fanned his face. "And might Ti I, mention Perseffor Mantu…this very morn made honor Group member…he now…'*Hammer*'." He laboriously raised a finger for each man in the room. "We… now…*four!*"

Mack zoned out, savoring the nickname. "…Hammer…" The astronomer's whole face lit up, and he embraced Amantu like a long-lost friend. "Dubious congratulations, Professor! And I apologize for inconveniencing you on the holiday: I don't make a habit of ringing strangers. That said, I want to thank you from the bottom of my heart for making a hole in your schedule, and sincerely beg your forgiveness regarding the untoward treatment en route. This must all seem a most unfunny holiday prank. I assure you, it is not."

"*You*…you wish to thank *me?* Sir, when my students

learn of our association I will be all but unapproachable."

"So you shall, so you shall." Mack drummed his palms on his thighs. "All right, then." He leaned to Izzy's tray, poured himself some dark amber spirit or other, and addressed the room with his glass. "For the last several years I've been chasing these exceedingly faint signals, totally unrelated to the waves I'm used to handling. They were some kind of magnetic residue, here one minute, gone the next. I had the deuce of a time, but once I'd sampled and digitized a specimen I found myself studying a terrestrial wave pattern—yet one that was electrically inverted; what I've come to know as a 'waveprint.' By accident, I had it played back in A/V. So here I was, absolutely certain I'd detected the path of an exotic new particle. Imagine my expression when I picked out the distinct sawing of my shaving razor.

"I put out a seek right away, hoping the lens could find more specimens, and then—oh, what a floodgate I've opened."

Mack set down his drink and forcibly folded his hands. "I tried to run in time, but I was too slow; I was infernally slow. One day I sold a few scans to the university and used the proceeds to purchase an axon accelerator off the black market. I got…close with the skin. Real close. I will confess to becoming addicted. I allowed it to vivisect my virtual brain."

Abel coughed loudly. Amantu discretely fingered a golden hem. Izzy angrily wolfed his drink. "There go party."

"Gentlemen," Mack said. "My sins are off my chest." He rose philosophically. "Now to the order of business. We all know that thought is merely a process; that the 'mind,' when it comes right down to it, is actually a *verb*, as opposed to that *noun* we so familiarly call the 'brain.' Our comprehension, our emotions, our memories, are utterly reliant upon the living brain. When the body dies the brain stops, and when the brain stops the mind ceases to exist. As I say, we know all this. But when the skin apprehended it—that a man's mind is unbounded potential, as opposed to the closed and predictable thing it was used to running in—it began processing my thoughts as electrical phenomena exclusive of real time." Mack nodded at the room. "Mind-reading isn't as far-fetched as it sounds, you guys. Not when it's a program doing the reading. Let me elaborate." He made a frame of his hands. "At any given moment a brain is active, there're tens of thousands of synaptic clefts working synchronously, and the impulses jumping those gaps produce minute discharges the skin digitizes. Sampled instantaneously, they create an instantaneous pattern—an image, a feeling, a thought. In real time, they correspond to a continuous series of seamless mental images. So we could say, metaphorically, the living brain's a theater, the mind's a motion picture, and those tens of thousands of firing synapses are pixels—pulses that are read, digitized, and mapped by Solomon, the skin-written program you're about to meet.

"Solomon cross-references radially, rather than linearly, so a runner gets momentary access to a whole world of inform-ation. Literally. Not by painstakingly seeking it out, mind you, but by allowing the program free access to his head. Solomon finds what *you* want. And sometimes a whole lot more. How much more? Just listen:

"Any occurrence outside a vacuum, no matter how subtle, produces a current in its supporting medium—for ex-ample, the vibrations of my voice are reaching your eardrums via the intervening air. Every cluster of waveprints, whether produced by my vocal cords right now or by some miscel-laneous rockslide half a million years ago, is unique, and can be reproduced, by Solomon here: reconstructed and digitally saved, to be studied at leisure by his runner. That's because those currents are producing discrete magnetic profiles that are 'encoded' in our planet's gravitational field in real time. Acting as a super-sensitive receiver, Solomon's able to pick out and transpose those collected profiles—'decode' them—and convert them back to pulses that disrupt the medium of air, thereby reproducing the clusters, which in turn stimulate our tympanic membranes."

"Doctor Mack." Amantu clasped his hands and cocked his head; a move so characteristic it compelled immediate mim-icking from both Izzy and Abel. "Please correct me if I am in error. You are claiming your thoughts and your program's repository are in sync while the program is electromagnetically mirroring your synaptic activity?"

"Not just me. Whoever's running in Solomon at the time. And it doesn't have to be straightforward pulse transposition. Solomon's voice-sensitive. He can read and bookmark vocal commands linearly, without having to deal with all the normal peripheral autonomic mental activity."

The men fiddled with their drinks. Izzy grumbled, "Some name...Saw...Sawla. Strange. I—"

"The venerated name of a wise king who ruled thirty-five hundred years ago. There were lots of these so-called sacrosanct names."

Abel cuffed the psychoanalyst upside his head. "Ah, for Christ's sake, Izzy! You just had to ask, didn't you?"

"There you go. What does 'for Christ's sake' mean, Josh?"

"It's a meaningless interjection. Don't play with me, Ti."

"Well, what if I told you that that particular meaningless interjection pertained to a figure of great historical significance, and that most personal names do, as well? 'Israel,' for example, is pivotal; the name of an ancient kingdom in the Eastern Hemisphere. All our names—Abel, Titus, Moses—are of great fame and antiquity."

"Then *'for Christ's sake!'* I second my own interjection! *'Israel'* is the nom de plume of our skeptical little friend here, and those three syllables have no significance whatsoever. He could have been named 'Bugaboo,' and he'd still be the same inimitable irritant we all know and love. You're reading too much out of your data, Ti. Besides, any fool can argue an abstraction."

Mack bowed and swept an arm. "Just so. Ladies and gentlemen, I give you...*Solo.*"

The house lights came down and the chamber was permeated by a lazily swirling field, so tenuous the skin behind showed distinctly. Mack furrowed his brow, and his guests could have sworn the field discreetly funneled his way. A frantic ruckus began just outside. The voices of the Group burst into the room, accompanied by the noise of their violent entry and a sound like the pop-and-hiss of escaping air. Moments later Abel could be heard shouting, his voice seeming to issue from an unoccupied space: "It's only us, Titus! Sorry about the racket! Slight disagreement with your neighbors! Happy New

Year!" Then the muffled response: "And to! Just give me a minute! Help yourselves!"

The wispy field vanished and the lights came back up.

Abel nodded slyly. "Happy New Year, indeed! Gentlemen, we've been acoustically monitored, probably from the moment we hit the porch. A clever bit of hopping about with the audio, but…c'mon, Ti. Something a tad more sophisticated."

"Fair enough, Josh. What's running isn't a one-dimensional read. Example: as steady fields of broadcast energy, natural and artificial light register constant values. Solomon perfunctorily enters and ignores such values as structurally insignificant. However, wherever a constant value is interrupted by an opaque object Solomon reads a reduction. A plane surface will render equal reductive values over its breadth, and so be interpreted as flat. On the other hand, a complex surface, such as a man's face, will produce countless variations in values— values Solomon automatically translates as pixels to produce three-dimensional imagery. Likewise color, depth, perspective—infinite degrees in variation are instantaneously mapped and reproduced as images readily accessible to our humble rods and cones. A quick demonstration should suffice. The program opens with a single password; his nickname. The tones comprising 'Solomon' mean nothing. I had to write it in that way or he'd be all over the place whenever those three syllables were innocently spoken. His runner's thoughts are accessed the instant he's activated. Observe." Cocking his head, he said, "Solo."

The lights dimmed. Once more those voices exploded into the room, this time accompanied by a trio of sheer apparitions. It was the Group again, falling all over one another. Amantu's intense likeness raced right through him while, not two feet away, the three-dimensional image of Abel scrambled to its feet, held a transparent sleeve to one nostril, and called out, "It's only us, Titus! Sorry about all the racket! Slight disagreement with your neighbors! Happy New Year!"

The field retracted and the lights came up.

Abel applauded generously. "Boys, boys, boys! We've been scanned as well as scammed. Don't let your guards down for a minute! And my objection stands, Titus. All you've done is elaborate on an illusion. A visual recording, no matter how adroitly orchestrated, is still just a technological display."

"Not so. I couldn't possibly have incorporated Solomon's range of detail. Solo. The Battle of the Little Bighorn."

Broad daylight displaced the interior lighting. The overhead skin's dome was now sky-blue. The gel tiles uncannily resembled dirt and bare pasturage, while the skin proper appeared to have been replaced by open horizon. The Group were standing on a wide plain surrounded by reddish bluffs and craggy canyons. Close enough to touch, huddling cavalrymen crouched behind their steeds, discharging rustic firearms while naked savages hacked at them with stick-mounted stones. The action was so realistic everybody but Mack hit the deck.

"Solo. Break." The fighting figures dissolved.

The men picked themselves up slowly, amazed and embarrassed. Faint traces of kicked dirt still appeared to hang in the air.

"Those—" Amantu marveled, "those were *horses!*"

"So they were, Hammer. What we're seeing is actual history, not the prettified stuff we've been taught."

"To which I say bravo! See how he uses titillating images to lead us from analysis? Hear how convincingly they clatter? It's all a heap of technological legerdemain."

"Titus..." Amantu faltered. "Your zeal is admirable. However, sir, I am thoroughly learned in Western history. Were I not so moved by your sincerity I would doubtless get comfortable and 'enjoy the show.' But here I must object. I feel I can accurately describe our past over thirteen millennia. These images are without foundation."

"But can you *show* me?"

The ghost of a chuckle. "If you mean, can I produce dramatic photographic imagery in three dimensions, along with realistic acoustics, well..."

"That's exactly what I mean. Try for yourself."

Amantu cleared his throat.

"Just remember to use the pass."

All eyes were on him. Amantu very clearly enunciated, "So low." He hesitated in the sudden glimmer of drifting fireflies. "Reveal All Hall's Congress. Year 817, Month November,

Day Eleven. It would have been a Tuesday."

The skin now presented a wide flowing parade of film clips, accompanied by thin bites of atonal audio. The clips were obviously contrived; acted out and edited, stuffed with period costumes and unconvincing sets.

"Solo," Mack said. "Break." The fireflies disappeared.

"Defective," Amantu pronounced.

"Not at all. In reality no such event took place."

"I stand vindicated," Abel objected. "Those were educational films; I recognized at least two of 'em."

"That's all Solomon has to draw on. That and voluminous fabricated records. The Text Alone command, when applied to the skin, would turn this place into a spherical encyclopedia. But in projected T/A, molecules in the air are vibrated to mimic pixels, creating distinct alphanumeric patterns. Solo. Today's date. Text Alone."

Characters two feet high by a foot wide, misty-white and resembling steam, appeared hovering at eye-level:

1 JANUARY 2509

Mack took a broad step to the side. The characters swiveled to face him. He hopped back, and the display followed suit. "The program's also voice-sensitive to its runner. In heavy research, hearing a real-time response does wonders. Solo. Today's date, in V/S."

Titus Mack's own voice responded, from the same general space as the dissolving characters:

"January First, Twenty-Five Oh Nine."

His eyes gleamed. "Then again, you'd get that same film-like response if you requested skin text files on something called the Emancipation Proclamation and a fellow named Lincoln. But in A/V we get related graphics. Solo. Antietam. September 17, 1867. Real Time."

A melee erupted in the center of the room, blew onto the enveloping skin, and quickly metastasized throughout the apparent horizon. Suddenly hundreds of uniformed men were grappling tooth and nail, firing antique weapons, stabbing one another with short mounted sabers. An echoless cannonade issued from "distant" standing guns and from "nearby" hand-held artillery.

"Solo. Break." The house lights came up and the raging soldiers dissolved. "Something called the American Civil War. On that single day over twenty-five thousand men fell in mortal combat." Mack looked at Amantu quizzically. "As I understand it, they were in disagreement over a matter of color."

The professor returned the look. "Solo. Parsominius Beale. Year Nine-Two-Nine. The particle driver prototype. Real Time."

Images of Beale, or a man supposed to be Beale, rolled round the skin, accompanied by tinny narration.

"Solo. Jack the Ripper. London, England. September Seventh, 1888. 2300 hours."

A dark foggy night. The Group were standing on a side-walk bordering a narrow cobblestone street, facing a cul-de-sac. Dripping brick buildings loomed to either side, lit fitfully by lamps that seemed to tilt with the perspective. A heavily made-up woman was sauntering toward them, her low white dress clinging, a nervous smile on her flushed cockney face. She came up to Izzy and Amantu swinging her little sequined purse, her eyes sparkling. When she was almost upon them a man stepped between them from behind, kissed her once, clamped a hand over her mouth and cleanly slit her throat. As though in a dance, he swept her into an alley between two dirty gray buildings.

"Solo. Break."

Izzy looked away. "Bloody little world you dug up."

Mack studied Amantu through his eyelashes. "So tell me, Professor, in all your research have you ever come across the name Sam Butcher?"

"Unfamiliar," Amantu admitted.

"How about the Hard Left? The Messiah Commission? The Black Days?"

"That—" Amantu said excitedly. "'Black Days!' Mentioned frequently in recall sessions. You can access such an event?"

"Solo. The Black Days. Winter of 2118." He looked up, annoyed. "Anywhere. Surprise me."

A different street, a different hemisphere, another century. It was the dead of night. Orion's belt winked cheerlessly on the overhead skin. The projected road was deserted, the neighborhood gutted. Every house was shut down, the streetlamps shot out. But in the distance could be seen several torches, approaching slowly, accompanied by the barks and whines of savage dogs.

"Not safe to walk alone," Mack commented. "Dangerous for the military also." He began to pace and, eerily, the domed enclosure appeared to roll right along. "Anyone in a uniform was likely as not to have his brains blown out or his legs chewed off. This was real guerilla warfare. Solo. Stop." The entire projection froze instantly. Stars ceased blinking, torches became orangey spikes of light. In this mode the tongues of flame lost their natural look, turning into tiny serrated prominences with obvious peaks and shelves. Conversely, the stars no longer showed their characteristic atmospheric winking. They were positive-value pinpricks; ice-cold holes in the electromagnetic field.

"Over four hundred years ago, the Eastern and Western Hemispheres were engaged in a bloody war that employed the oceans, the atmosphere, and eventually space itself. Back then there was something known as 'hard copy,' which meant that records were stored materially. Believe it or not, most data could be accessed by just about anybody. Much of that data was unclassified, of course—homely stuff for basic education and entertainment. But it was right out in the open, and these continents' borders were so porous your best friend could easily have been your worst enemy; at one time it was estimated that the ratio of citizen-to-foreign agent was roughly one-to-one. Our enemies were communicating internally by a method known as 'effacement.' In this process, bound leaves of paper are subtly graven in a manner invisible to the naked eye, but readily picked out by a trained agent. All a man had to do was go to a 'library' or 'newspaper rack,' locate an adroitly dog-eared 'book' or 'newspaper,' and use a special, pressure-sensitive cloth to obtain orders or pass on intelligence.

"Our solution was to scan all data, then destroy every bit of the old hard copy. Logic held that saved public-use data could be reprinted at war's end, while classified data remained encrypted. But by war's end technology had perfected scrollers and IBCs. The average man had access to more information than all the world's universities and museums combined. Hard copy had become obsolete.

"Now, I'm telling you this because it pertains strongly to what you're about to learn. That original hard copy held historical data accrued from the dawn of civilization. It was the written record of all that we are, and the sacred history of ancient peoples in the Eastern Hemisphere. Our laws and mores were built around the worship of their divinity. Citizens were tortured, armies perished. Whole states rose and fell in the name of this imaginary ruler."

"Here we go again! And just when I thought we were getting real."

"I didn't say it was real, Josh. I said it was imaginary."

"Then," demanded Amantu, "you are claiming that international conflict, rather than plague-driven insanity, was responsible for these Black Days. You are prepared to prove this?"

"There is no plague, Professor, and insanity is insanity. The history we've grown up with is a lie. You're all free to watch and come to your own conclusions. Consider this my New Year's gift."

"Then drop the divinity hogwash, and let's just relax and enjoy ourselves. We're not rubes, Ti. And as far as your new toy goes, blaze away. But bear in mind that a lifetime of practical experience will never be undone by a roomful of clever imaging."

"Examine these records for yourself, Josh. You'll see that a whole continent full of schemers couldn't produce all the data Solomon can access. It would take millennia—damn it, it *did* take millennia!" He poked a cocky forefinger at the professor's chest. "I'm telling you, 'Hammer,' you and I'll become the best of friends. You'll have a blast here; the same jaw-dropping joyride I've been on for months. Solo. The Black Death. Overhead Sweep."

And the room was all azure sky, with two hundred feet of apparent air where the floor used to be. Miles and miles of rolling countryside made up the seeming far-below. A quiet world; just primitive villages, winding dirt roads, and woods interspersed with hills and streams. A few walled cities could be seen, heavily guarded by sentries. Adjoining roads were block-aded or dug up. "Over a thousand years ago," Mack went on, "our forebears had a plague of their own. The disease that depopulated the world below us was of the bubonic-pneumonic variety. I've seen fields littered with the corpses of cattle and sheep, houses deliberately burned to the ground, carts porting bloated human remains. I had Solomon cross-reference the A/V with subsequent related clusters. Rat fleas were the vectors. Back then sanitation was a terrible problem, and medicine prac-tically nonexistent. Solo. The 'Satellite Frays.' Deep Zoom. Fast Motion."

The chamber was now a hemispheric module in the upper stratosphere, with the visual panorama and technological feel of an orbiting observation station. The infinite black gran-deur, brilliant with a billion white stars, was eclipsed by a dizzying video game-like battle between batteries of globular satellites. Mirror-plated orbiters took hits, automatically spun to return fire, spun back. This was a robotic war, viewed at an accelerated rate. True to the absence of a medium, the crystal-clear visual was absolutely soundless. "Solo. Ground Zero, Hiroshima, August Sixth, 1945. Real Time. Zoom Out."

A piece of sun shot up from a coastal city and blew out into a hot smoky umbrella. There came a blinding flash that did not blind, followed by a stunning rumble that grew into a tidal roar. A raging wall of water swallowed the room as if it were a sea polyp. And, though it sounded for all the world like a giant had just stepped on the place, the contents of the room were entirely unaffected.

"Solo. Break." Mack spun around. "What did I tell you!"

Abel shook his head sadly. "1945? Come on, Ti. Why not 9945?"

"Balls descending!" Izzy wheezed. "Could've swear. Entire city...wipe out!"

Amantu faced his host critically. "I am unclear. How does all this pertain to your summons of yesterday? I will concede to a genuine fascination with the visual proceedings. However, this is not history. It is an impertinent series of sophisticated projections, which, albeit convincing in their breadth and drama, titillate without validation."

"But this *is* history, Professor. I didn't bring you all the way out here just for a light show. And as to pertinence; every fact, no matter how insignificant, pertains to every other fact." Mack drummed his fingers on the drink stand. "Look, let me take you guys *back*—all the way to the dawn of actual history. Not that history recorded by scribes and geologists, but to the Original recall event; a calamity so devastating it became imprinted for good in our collective consciousness. It was," Mack said, "our first great memory as a species." He nodded. "Solo. The Deluge. Step Back ten seconds and Stand in Still Motion until Mark."

The skin was washed in daylight. The phantom horizon expanded. And expanded, and expanded; adding layers of apparent distance in zooms meted out hexadecimally. The theater of Solomon was now a primitive, temperate arena that went on forever in every direction.

"To all appearances we are standing in the Eastern Hemisphere, in Northern Africa, in a vast basin that prehistoric man, had he the wits about him, would have designated the Mediterranean Valley. It's the place where we started; the cradle of man. We'd barely gone from grunts to syllables, but we were true men, not progenitors. Here's where homo sapiens sapiens tribalized, under a fair sky, with no end to tomorrow. Sorry, fellows. Civilization didn't break out in the Upper West, fostered by a line of secular scientists under the happiest of circumstances.

"In the Mediterranean the potential was limitless. Gathering accommodated hunting. There were laws, there were taboos, there were incentives for growth; intellectual, spiritual, economic. As mammals we grouped, and as men we expanded. As a tribe we extended to the very limits of that great valley.

"One day the Inevitable caught up with us. The Atlantic Ocean had been worrying at the Valley's natural western barrier for millennia. It was eaten away only gradually, of course, but the tide pool became a seething reservoir. Something had to give, and when it did it was on a scale grand even by terran standards." Mack turned to the west skin. "Gentlemen. I suggest you hang onto your bladders. Solo. Mark."

Immediately the room filled up with the sound of thunder. The floor seemed to pound away like a thrashing beast, though the Group's feet remained firmly planted. Even the sky appeared to shake. Then, almighty spectacle, a wide blue horror came crashing out of the west. Walls of water flew hundreds of feet high, left and right, so vast they appeared to leap along in slow motion. When the howling monster arrived, the impression of impact was so realistic it all but knocked the Group off their feet.

"Solo. Stop!"

The observatory was swallowed up in blue. But not a static blue. All around the men, pixel streaks showed a frozen turmoil, electronically indicating air displaced, earth dispatched, fluid dispelled.

"Solo. Zoom out. Deep Overview, Wide Pan. Fast Motion Times Ten."

All that blue was instantly replaced by air. The planet fell away with a sound like air through a straw, atmospheric particulates appearing to granulate in the rapid remapping of data. The Group stood in apparent suspension, staring down between their feet. Mack's zodiacal floor showed the Mediterranean Valley, now partitioned by unsteady lines of grid, irresistibly on its way to becoming the Mediterranean Sea. They watched the brown-and-green basin being covered by an inching blue carpet, even at this rate looking like it would take forever.

Their narrator's voice was dreamlike. "The human race was nearly extinguished. Only those folks nearest the rim had time to get out. They spread across the virgin land; over the ages those in the north growing fairer due to the higher latitudes, those moving down the African continent developing darker characteristics. The ones migrating eastward retained our basic stock's brownness and propensity to swart. But the catastrophe was firmly established in our subconscious. In almost all cultures there exists this legend of a Great Flood, which destroyed the 'World.' Also, there are innumerable references to obliterated fabulous sites; among them an 'Eden,' likely man's first homestead, and an island called 'Atlantis' that was forever submerged. The big exception to these ensconced Flood fables is the Orient, which developed collaterally."

Mack looked into Amantu's eyes. "Professor Amantu, cultural recall is a hybrid phenomenon; a combination of *a)*: evolutionary changes brought about in the brain as a special extension of the self-preservation instinct, and *b)*: mental adaptation coerced by tribal lore enforced over generations."

Amantu nodded appreciatively.

"Solo. The 'Holy Land'." The scene "below" instantly shifted to the Mediterranean Sea's easternmost crescent. "What we're now observing is far more recent; a scant twenty-five centuries ago. It's the roots of Western commercial civilization. There were two superpowers; in the north an empire known as Babylonia, and to the south the great dynastic state of Egypt. Solo. Highlight." The mentioned waveclusters took on an amber glow. "The natural trade route was a thin strip of land between the Mediterranean on our left, and that blue line to the right, the Dead Sea.

"In those days there were wooly ruminants known as 'sheep,' used both for their wool and as food. Their handlers were called 'shepherds.' One of these shepherds, a man named Abram, took up husbandry on that strip of land and became the patriarch of several tribes called 'Israel'—and there's the origin of our dear bobbing colleague's name. Well, as you can imagine, these tribes were not amenable to those superpowers' commercial flux, nor were they about to move. When things got sticky, the Egyptian kingpin neatly solved the problem by relocating Abram's entire clan to a prison in Babylonia. There they were left to rot, an utterly vanquished people, for nigh on fifty years. But while there, their jailers entertained them with a crude old Babylonian legend about a so-called 'Messiah'."

Here Amantu had to object. "Sir—"

"Please, Hammer. Just call me Ti."

The professor seethed. "*Sir*, forgive me, but I find this line of expression dangerously close to snatching."

Mack took a swallow and emphatically shook his head. "Uh-uh, my friend. No. I beg your patience; I'm simply defining the mindset directly responsible for the illusion we labor under today. Nobody will be snaught on my watch. As it stands, I'm already condensing like crazy." He blew out a sigh. "Now, when those prisoners were released, they yearned only to return to their homeland. A great leader named Moses—and there's your bid, Professor—shepherded them thereto, and represented them in their further misadventures with the head Egyptian. They claimed an elite status with their divinity, decried the Egyptian's divinity as a dirty fraud, and insisted their almighty divinity could whip the Egyptian's puny divinity any day of the week.

"Okay. In due time a great empire called Rome dominated affairs around the Mediterranean. By then Abram's diehard descendants had established grazing states that were in direct conflict with the imperial Roman political system. These were some barbaric times. The homesteaders were subjected to all kinds of unmentionable persecutions.

"A local prophet, their 'messiah,' attained great fame as an orator. Since his series of sermons were uncompromisingly system-damning, the empire made a particularly tragic example of him. As I said, these were barbaric times. It was all too much for this proud, much-subjugated people. Unable to retaliate militarily, they capitalized on their prophet's execution by propagating stories of a divine connection, and proclaimed their people would rise in his name and, with the supernatural legerdemain of their wrathful God, appropriate the planet in his honor.

"Gentlemen, this campaign was no caprice. It reigned for over twenty-one centuries, in the process shaking governments, felling armies, and radically altering uncountable lives. Solo. The Second Crusade."

In an instant a ragtag army was trudging through the observatory, leading trains of marchers, followers, and pack animals without end. Several naked and scourged individuals were shouldering wooden crosses ten feet high and half as broad.

"Solo. Tomas de Torquemada."

The blink of an eye, and an old man in dark robes was standing in the Group's midst, watching dispassionately while a screaming woman burned at the stake in a walled dirt field. The skin's phantom horizon produced throbbing checkerboard patterns where flames rose above the crude wall into sunlight. There was a brief and very chilly interlude, when the inquisitor turned and appeared to glare at Amantu. False firelight made his wizened face a splotchy death mask.

"Solo. Flagellants. A specimen."

A pack of frenzied men danced around the room, flogging themselves with whips, slats, and birch rods. They screamed hysterically while flailing, tossing their heads like demented children. It was hard to tell if they were enjoying the ritual or merely crying out for the attention of their peers.

"Solo. Break."

Abel shook his head in the familiar soft white light. "You've shown us nothing, Ti. All we've seen is a freak show reminiscent of a thousand carrier tales."

But Mack just smiled. "Izzy, do you think you could manage another tray?" He called up chairs and cigars. "There's stuff to munch on in the galley, and Solomon'll run the heat or air if it gets uncomfortable. The lavatory's right through that port, so if anybody's gotta go, please do so now. Because this is just about to get interesting."

Chapter Five

History Lesson

When the butts were situated and the tumblers all tall, Mack buffed his palms and turned to Amantu. "Now for the main event. This is especially for you, Hammer. But even if Solomon's data comes off as incredible, I think it's safe to say we'll all agree that the experience is worth our full and erudite attention."

Abel's eyes gleamed. "And I think it's safe to say we expected nothing less."

"Solo. Samuel Obadiah Butcher. The Republican Convention of 2116. Still Motion."

The skin immediately reconfigured. The men were now standing in an apparent chamber of four right-angled apparent walls ninety feet apart: Mack's roomy observatory had become a packed auditorium. A thousand black-robed, black-brimmed statues were crammed inside this huge teak-and-mahogany image of a room, each one mesmerized by a gaunt, fierce-eyed elderly man behind a cruciform podium on a backlit stage.

"Sam Butcher," Mack said evenly. "The Republican Party's man of the hour. Raised in a famous evangelical family, 'The Barnstorming Butchers,' as I recall. Born entertainer, stand-up orator, and multimillionaire at forty. As patriarch of a bay-to-cape web of Faith Families, he attacked the Americas' moral decay with venom and resolve."

"Ven-ge..." Izzy sputtered. "I...gevenny...*what?* Clarify, man! Even-*who*-ical?"

"Evangelical. Back-formation of the word 'angel,'

meant to signify a supernatural agent of the pre-Colonial divinity. *Evangelists* were the forerunners of our modern snatchers. But this was way before telepresence. The evangelism of Butcher's day was a perfectly legal system promoting the tenets of a globally-accepted supreme being's teaching, complete with aggressive campaigning and ritualistic behavior."

Abel slapped his knees. "Oh, please."

"Now wait a minute, AJ. These people were sincere. What's more, they were desperate. There'd been a deep schism in the machinery of democracy for forty years, with liberals and conservatives leaning ever farther from the middle; the left wing becoming the Hard Left and the right wing the Hard Right, the former growing deliberately dirtier in retaliation to the vaunted spotlessness of the latter. Our political system was in civil war. And with the election nearing, fully half the population were ready to fight to the death for Mister Butcher here, while the other half were rowdily impassioned over their candidate. Solo. Harry Riser. Two hours later. Still Motion."

The black-garbed statues dissolved like men of foam. In their place arose an equal number of men and women, all outrageously coiffed and costumed. Many were nearly naked, wearing only scraps of flesh-tone underwear strung with bizarrely-dyed feathers and lewdly-shaped baubles. By their posture it was evident they'd been captured in a highly suggestive dance. Up onstage, a chubby beaming man posed like a gaudy gift to humanity.

"Harry Riser was a gadabout, a publicity hound and, well, quite frankly, a flaming homosexual. He represented a popular interpretation of the constitution that equates liberty with license—as though the meaning of a free society is getting away with all you can. There's no doubt that under any other circumstances he and his hedonistic circus would have been laughed into obscurity, but the Hard Right represented something that, to freemen everywhere, was even more unpalatable: the utter annihilation of that hard-won liberty. A week before the election the consensus was plain: the Left was going to win in a landslide. Sam Butcher was shouted down and threatened, his speeches parodied and his platform ridiculed. At the close of the campaign he was all but impotent."

Izzy considered the crowd through his glass, his head rocking left and right. "But...Gad, man! Was no—middle ground?"

"None. The pendulum had swung too far. Now skip a beat. Mysterious rumors surface alleging improprieties between Riser and a retarded boy; a boy whose mother boasted a red-letter reputation with congressmen and various welfare personnel. Although this woman is reported receiving a million dollars from unnamed sources before evaporating from public view, it's already too late for Riser. A kind of tribal rage against child molestation takes the mind of man and media. Rider is hounded, assaulted, placed under full Secret Service protection. The Butcher camp leap on the moment like piranha. Sam's eleventh-hour slogan trembles on every lip: 'Cop or con, man or child; *no one* likes a pedophile!' Riser is consigned to the bowels of history. Solo. Harry Riser. Two days Forward. Real Time."

An instant later the men were outdoors. All those dancing statues had been replaced by a wildly screaming mob of frenetic projections, blowing in and out of focus as they ran. Fists passed through Abel's and Amantu's gaping faces while Izzy scrambled under nonexistent feet. The din-and-flurry was so realistic it all but obscured a phalanx of riot police fighting to escort a haunted-looking Riser to safety.

"Solo. Break." Mack clasped his hands behind his back and absently watched his guests recover. "Now, Butcher did win the presidency, but less by electoral college than by acclamation. As things turned out, we'd all have been a lot better off if they'd just stuck with Riser.

"Sam was a born showman with a tremendous ego. His speeches became sermons, his Oval Office objections outright chastisements. He turned the highest office on the planet into his personal pulpit. This was too much for the Senate and House.

"Butcher was impeached, found mad, and removed unto the wailing bereavement of over a billion 'Little Butchers.' His Vice bailed out right behind him. The interim rule of the House Speaker was so deliberately neutral the man was nicknamed the 'Plain Vanilla President.'

"Butcher began wandering across the country, preaching from the stage of a motorized sound system. Solo. The 'Soul Tsunami.' Overhead Zoom. Real Time."

The skin's phantom horizon gave way to hills crawling with people. The Group again received the distinct impression of observing from on high, though their feet remained in direct contact with Mack's floor. The big difference between this scene and Solomon's Black Death rendition was the level of activity—the mob 'below' was beyond belief; blue hills black with millions of followers, all crammed about the tiny creeping dot that was the rolling stage bearing Samuel Obadiah Butcher. The Group could hear him hollering over a powerful public address system; of repentance and remittance, of demons slain in virtuous battle.

"Sam knew how to hold a crowd; he used repetition to keep them in a trancelike state. This was one of the oldest tricks in the evangelical book. Listen to how he uses a simple sing-song phrase, '*Oh Soul*,' to control pheromonal output and blood pressure. Solo. Locate a Tsunami Chant. Enhance the Butcher audio file."

The scene shifted to late afternoon. Now Butcher's voice came through with exceptional clarity, while the mass responses of the crowd sounded as though on a separate track.

"Oh *Soul* of the burning night!"

"*Oh Soul!*"

"Oh *Soul* of the deepest sea!"

"*Oh Soul!*"

"Oh *Soul*, do *we*, cry *un*-to *thee!*"

"*Oh Soul! Oh Soul!*"

Mack was noting his friends' puzzled expressions while the chant progressed. "Solo. Stop." The mob froze, though its rhythm and passion still filled the room. "A 'soul'," Mack explained, "was a supposed entity, non-corporeal, that departed a cadaver to join the divinity in its otherworldly domain. It was essentially one's consciousness, freed from the unclean body for purification in an 'afterlife.' A neat trick if you can pull it off: mental immortality. As expressed in Tsunami philosophy, 'soul *of*' meant the deity itself; kind of a universal entelechy."

Abel laughed appropriately, but Amantu mused, "Rather

like a signature, albeit one infused with self-will."

Mack kneaded his chin. "Y'know, Hammer, you're a funny guy. A dynamic signature!" He winked at Abel. "Anyway, to stir up this kind of feeling was to waken a potentially wild animal, one that could go into stampede-mode at the drop of a hat. So from their earliest barnstorming days the Butchers had kept an ensemble of bodyguards; as much family as employees. By the time of the Tsunami, Sam was abundantly aware of his own mortality. Solo. Zoom in on Security. Real Time." Solomon instantly magnified a bare ring surrounding the slowly proceeding stage. Within this ring were hundreds of burly men, stepping back and forth, turning on their toes while staring into the crowd with looks of exaggerated menace. Security wore black shovel hats, very dark sunglasses, plush sable-lined parkas, black paratrooper pants, black combat boots. Each sloping hat bore a slender white cross emblazoned on its crown. Continuing this theme were bolo ties designed to resemble long white dangling crucifixes over black rayon dress shirts. Whenever these men turned, and they turned often, similar bone-white crosses could be seen running down the backs of their parkas; vertical beams corresponding to spines, horizontals to outstretched arms. "Mark well those men. They, and their descendants, play a pivotal role in the fun to come.

"Everywhere Butcher paused, this astounding entourage halted with him. Whole cities erupted on these sites, bearing strange names like Davidtown, Miracle House, Jericho Junction. Some still exist. That entourage included media of every level and caliber, National Guardsmen and special agents, sympathizers and camp followers, the dysfunctional and the dispossessed. And, thanks to those media, the details of his movements spread like wildfire. Finally Butcher, claiming to be directed by a voice on high, staked his claim in an area known as Kentucky, now the Colony-proper's dead-center. He named this area New Nazareth, and it became a magnet for millions upon millions of citizens from every coast. There was no way on earth to take care of sanitation in such a situation. A hardy breed of field rat came out of the hills and ran rampant in the garbage and half-buried fecal matter. Sexually-transmitted diseases went unchecked. The place began to look more like a battlefield than a mass celebration, and soon death walked boldly among the faithful. The Guard and Crosses worked heroically, the rats were fought with cleavers and gate wire, but in the end it was Butcher's charisma that held everybody together. The worse it got, the more they saw Sam as their savior. These were some odd times. In all major cities, his supporters erected supply lines, darkened the windows of their houses, and walked around dressed entirely in black, making no secret of their allegiance. At the same time, perfectly stable citizens were quitting their jobs and selling their homes, packing up their families and joyously crossing the country to support the Tsunami. Solo. Break." The lights came up.

"Gentlemen, this was no fad or public caprice. So far as the government was concerned, the Soul Tsunami's mass migration was tantamount to anarchy." Mack stabbed a forefinger in the air to make his points. "Minimally, its effects were a staggered economy, a breakdown of law and order, and a dramatic increase in civil polarization.

"The Hard Left's abiding resentment over Riser's foiling, and their burning hatred of the Little Butchers' haughty divinity-worship, grew into a cult, the cult into a movement, and the movement into a crusade. There were some despicable beatings of those black-draped followers, right in public. Their children were ostracized, their wives ridiculed and sexually assaulted. Then in 2118, on a special divinity-holiday known as 'Christmas,' a coast-to-coast coalition of university students, goaded by rage, pharmaceuticals, and peer pressure, introduced a digital virus into every municipal mainframe. This virus, the so-called 'Messiah Bug,' instantly deleted every reference to religion. The divinity-worshippers' overpowering word of history and law, a two thousand year-old tome known as 'Bible,' was wiped from the annals of history in a heartbeat.

"My friends, it's impossible to overstate the effect this single act had upon millions and millions of human beings. Beyond outrage, beyond violation, beyond imagination—the record of all they believed and prized...gone! After an interim of shock the faithful went berserk, attacking anyone in uniform. They felt that the system, and that technology itself, were somehow to blame—that the government, having transferred all hard copy into a digital format, was directly responsible for the complete loss of their profound teaching. All over the continent, appliances in general, and digital devices in particular, were attacked with great vengeance. Fueled by religious sermons on every street corner, mobs dressed entirely in black stormed archives and governmental offices, smashing to pieces all equipment responsible for data storage and manipulation...for filtration, for power, for sewage. Officials—even minor bureaucrats—were torn limb from limb, buildings were burned to the ground. In their frenzy the faithful destroyed the foundation of their very survival.

"When word of the tome's deletion reached New Nazareth, the Little Butchers went through various stages of denial and hysteria before breaking down completely. Butcher himself collapsed as though struck by lightning. Once recovered, he claimed to have undergone some kind of subliminal interview with the divinity, who told him that prayer must not be a meek mumbling but a 'begging outcry.' And 'prayer,' in this context, means a vocal attempt to attract a busy divinity's attention. So the heart of New Nazareth bleated out its plaint, and the fringes joined in. The urgency went out in waves, until it seemed that every North American voice was involved. Throats were screamed bloody raw, women swooned, elderly men died in their passion.

"One night not long after, a divine vision appeared in New Nazareth for a period of just over eleven seconds before vanishing altogether. But it was enough to convince the Little Butchers that Sam was their 'New Messiah,' which meant he was, practically speaking, an heir in the divine line, essentially a second son of the divinity itself. Butcher thereupon wandered off in a trance, his path cleared by hundreds of thousands of scrabbling men and women. With millions more hard on his heels, he staggered up to Crystal Cave, the mouth of a vast underground caverns system, known, pre-Colony, as Mammoth. Standing in a sea of jabbering humanity, Sam informed a breathless world by video that his deity had ordered him to produce a new divine literature in their beloved old, centuries-tested hard copy, complete with an updated set of laws and admonitions. This work-of-works was to be known as the New

Faith, and its word was to be absolute, with Butcher's interpretation final. Additionally he, Samuel Obadiah Butcher, had
been divinely-directed to select a body of assistants. Solo.
Crystal Cave. Mark. Zoom out. Still Motion."

From an apparent rise some two hundred yards off the
Mammoth entrance, the Group watched Butcher standing in a
pose of beatific submission, his arms thrown high. So sensitive
to human viewpoint was Solomon that the contemporary observers were aligned in perfect juxtaposition with the proximate
projections, as opposed to those seemingly-smaller figures in
the "distance." At this magnification there were already
thousands upon thousands of men and women squeezed about
the Group, their eyes and hands raised passionately.

"Zoom Out times ten." The breadth of vantage increased
tenfold, showing countless ever-tinier people cascading to the
cave's mouth, now a black pinprick in the hills.

"Times one hundred." At this point the Group were
staring from high upon a relief map, yet still swallowed up by
raving humanity. Butcher and his new inner circle were but
mist. "You see what I mean? This is the effect religion had on
people. Solo. Zoom in. Slow Clock at Mark."

The perspective rocketed back to Mark, whereupon the
imagery moved along at a retarded rate. Butcher was turning in
slow motion, a thousand men and women in his wake. The women were all very comely, the men strapping and intimidating.
The mouth of Crystal Cave, really an antechamber to the
staggering Mammoth Caverns system, was blockaded by Butcher's security. Their uniform had evolved to meet the leader's
heady status. The men now wore hooded black leather trench
coats with elongated white crosses on the arms, fronts, and
backs. Black leather gloves, heavily studded black belts, black
steel-toed boots. The same huge shades covered their eyes, and
the same white crosses showed on the fronts of their hoods, but
now white paint representing vertical cross-beams ran down the
faces, foreheads-to-throats, and, in like fashion representing
horizontal cross-beams, across the mouths to the ears.

"Solo. Break. These people accompanying Butcher were
to be his personal attendants while he undertook the awesome
task of dictating the divinity's mighty word. He led them into a

dark and dangerous world, courageously calling out platitudes to an unseen deity, his arms encumbered by a pair of blank flat stones. The rats followed them down.

"Conditions were deplorable. Unfettered by the regulations of civilization, the baser aspects of human nature quickly took hold. The caverns became savage cloistered arenas, and Sam little more than a cartoonish father figure. Torches contributed a fearsome ambience, injuries went untreated, sickness and claustrophobia brought many to the brink of insanity. At the entrance, Security assured the anxious multitude that everything downstairs was just dandy, and stomped the daylights out of anybody who got too curious. Food came down in a fairly steady stream, but the scraps were thrown into miscellaneous passages to rot, and any old hole served for a toilet. As the diseases of antiquity reemerged, the dying were left screaming in the dark. The rats grew bolder. In time a cult of the rat grew, blending almost seamlessly with the ancient religious tenets Butcher had been trying so hard to preserve. Even though he was grandstanding bravely, everybody knew he was scared out of his wits. He realized he'd have to resurface eventually, and knew, too, that when he did he'd better have something pretty damned impressive to show the impatient millions. What he didn't know is that blind fate will always trump blind faith.

Chapter Six

Madame Rat

"**B**y now Sam was well into his eighties. His joints were wracked, his bowels shot, his mind going. But he was, after all, a man. The women he brought down with him were selected for their sexual attractiveness, as well as for their pliability. And he was a very, very scared little man. The males he'd picked were the biggest and dumbest he could find. Sam was counting on their loyalty, but in due course progressive senility made him clinically paranoid; afraid of his circle, afraid of the dark, afraid of his own security men. And, more than anything, deathly afraid of the next showing of his deity. Solo. The Honeycomb Heart. Still Motion."

The observatory's interior became a deep stone vault lit by standing torches, their eerie peaked flames frozen in space and time. On a rock stage stacked with rat skulls sat a decrepit, weary Sam Butcher, the picture of profound depression, surrounded by black-robed men holding black-leaved manuscripts with black-dyed covers made of human parchment. Behind these men, soot-painted nude women could be seen in apparent pantomime, their arms thrown out and their heads tossed back. The scene in front of that stage was a paused full-blown orgy; naked men and women flung on the dirt floor, their glistening flesh smeared with fresh soot. Others were chained to the walls or heaped semiconscious on the stage. Caught in the act of wading through all these bodies were Butcher's security men, whips and prods in their beefy gloved fists. Their black cloaks had evolved to meet the circumstances; they were now full-length hooded affairs with elastic bands that kept the faces prominent, and featured bone-white crosses down the chests, backs, and limbs. That white facial paint had expanded to cover the entire face, making Security's visages, with those ominous dark glasses now like eye sockets, uncannily similar to death's heads.

"Here the New Messiah held court, haunted by demons and doubts and the natural afflictions of the aged. And here he handed down the edicts he claimed were set forth by the divinity, while his conspiring circle of disciples—that somber group of barefooted men standing round him in the black hooded cloaks—entered his ravings in the secret ink of urine on the Black Book's leaves, freely mistranslating as they went along. Those brawny men with the prods and lashes are the elite remnants of his old security team, the infamous 'Butcher's Butchers,' seen here engaged in their holy work and favorite pastime: torturing those made demented by religious fervor. These guys' predecessors were recruited from prize fighters and heavyweight wrestlers; even in his early post-barnstorming days Butcher was fearful enough to require a measure of viciousness in his protection. When he reached icon-status he had to turn over the job of hiring to team members themselves, and they engaged in recruitment tactics that were all-out contests of strength and violence. Underground competitions—fights to the death—were initially held for the New Messiah's sake, then as gory entertainments to gratify the Butchers' own egos and sick tribal impulses. Solo. Real Time."

The women began to dance and writhe. The torches' flicking umbrae slid across their painted curves. Security plucked up random souls and punched them back down, engrossed by a strangely methodical form of brutality.

"At this point it was still important to keep up an imperious front. Butcher took his pesthole's loveliest crawler for queen; a petite, pallid, manipulative brunette temptress he pet-named 'Little Mother,' but who was known by the inmates as Black Mary. To please her, and to justify their intimacy, he had her written into the New Faith as his divinely-graced personal bodyguard. Then, when things got hotter, he proclaimed her the divinity's chosen executioner. Little Mary took to her task with zeal, using rat fangs as stilettos. This is the origin of all those legends about a plague passer, the underground's notorious 'Infector Mater.'

"Butcher fell wildly in love with this little porcelain pervert; demented as she was, demented as they all were. I say 'pervert' because the woman was a flat-out masochist, as well as a sadist. She could take as much punishment as she dished out—the one thing she couldn't take was sentiment. Sam could only gratify her with beatings, which were never quite ferocious enough. The circle were into it, Security were all thumbs-up; the ambience was one hundred percent encouragement. Somewhere in there he lost it completely. Butcher had his little rat-queen nailed to a cross on the divinity-channeling stage. There's a real symbolism to this act, which I'll show you guys in a minute. The people took to torturing Mary ritualistically, egged-on by her ecstatic screams. The Honeycomb rapidly evolved into a bloody madhouse.

"When Sam couldn't stand it any longer he took the only out open to him—he went into convulsions, claimed a revelation, and jabbered his way back to the surface. In front of the whole hemisphere he announced that the divinity had commanded him to lead the world in a Final Crusade. Solo. The Upcoming. Still Motion."

And they were back outside, on what must have been a very cold, very dark night. Hundreds of generator-operated searchlights stood trained on Crystal Cave, painting one patch of the skin a brilliant white without increasing the room's illuminative content a whit. Butcher was crouching amongst countless prostrated black-clothed followers, his arms wrapped round his torso. It didn't require sound and motion to illustrate the mob's wracked passion: the faces around the Group were maniacally contorted.

"According to the New Messiah, 'God' had declared war on the 'Devil'; the former being his omniscient personal bodyguard, the latter being pretty much everything that didn't conform to the niceties of Western religion. All technology was to be destroyed, along with everybody not of Butcher's 'Divine Phalanx.' A cushy immortality would come to those who died in righteous battle, eternal damnation to anyone who hesitated.

Butcher first commanded that the permanent National Guard encampments around New Nazareth be attacked by his hastily-organized Faith Catapult; really just a mad dash of shrieking followers wielding any weapons they could jerry-rig. Incredulous troops were slaughtered in the frenzy, and many thousands of Butcher's Catapult mortally injured in the stampede.

"The military's retaliation was swift and panicky. Units of the Army and Air Force cut the faithful down in their tracks, causing an hysterical three-day mass exodus into the bowels of Mammoth." He inclined his head and said, "Solo."

And they were caught in a riot. The observatory was filled with bright daylight, the air clotted by confused voices, the artificial horizon made fuzzy by the all-out frenzy of uncountable scrabbling followers. Flesh was scraped away by rock as men, women, and children squeezed screaming into Crystal. In the apparent distance, a few fighter jets and half a dozen attack helicopters circled for additional runs. The Group stood riveted as a pair of copters swept over the mob, spewing bullets that left pockets of humanity flopping. Amantu instinctively threw up his arms as a hammering column of lead tore through him and passed.

"Back down below," Mack said while the slaughter raged around them, "Butcher had to fight in the dark. He was a lousy general; almost every command he gave ended in a massacre. Solo. Stop. Meanwhile survivors continued to pile in, one on top of the other. Eventually they blocked off the entrance and turned the place into a wailing asylum. These interconnecting caverns are enormous—according to Solomon over three hundred and fifty miles long, and in some spots deep beyond measure. There were myriad uncharted breaks to the outside world, flues and the like, where locals were able to set up supply lines from the cities by tunneling around troops. Many of these excavations comprise the root system of our present-day Colony.

"The Army blew the blocked entrance to grit and poured inside. Butcher's people retreated one cavern for every lost battle, while he muttered and paced like some lunatic commander in a besieged bunker. Yet despite their New Messiah's delirium, or maybe because of it, they continued to fight savagely, relying on ambush, a secret code based on echoes, and a selfless will to engage that awed as much as frustrated the advancing soldiers. They were driven back by an antique, gasoline-based gel called 'napalm.' No one knew for sure if it was tunnel fever or tacit agreement—and Solomon is unable to pinpoint a direct order for me—but when the faithful were at last pressed into an unbelievably vast blind chamber, which also happened to be a natural crude basin, the troops, who were only to use their napalm as a means of prodding, turned all they had on Butcher and Company, incinerating the lot on the spot. I won't try your stomachs with *that* visual. The gale of data produces a highly distorted playback anyway. Solo. The Aftermath. Zoom Out."

New Nazareth on a dreary autumnal morn.

Files of body bags on stretchers, winding up a temporary road out of Crystal, en route to a series of makeshift hospitals separated by columns of troop transports. Helicopters hovering like dragonflies. Teams carrying out black-draped crates and litters heaped with miscellaneous items.

"All of New Nazareth was placed under quarantine. Uncounted survivors, guerrillas and the like, escaped into the hills, where they took to digging out tunnels in earnest, eventually hooking up with the supply lines and bringing in refugees from the cities. See all those boxes with the black covers? They contain cribs. Secure vaults were discovered in the depths, peopled only by nursemaids watching over infants in black swaddling cloths. Notes, written in urine on soot-coated rags, were pinned to these cloths with messages like, 'Please let little Nehemiah walk with the Lord,' et cetera. Solo. Stop."

The grim picture froze. Mack looked at the Group thoughtfully. "Solomon tabulated the body bags, using Fast Motion in a temporal Zoom mode. Forget exactitude: over five million, seven hundred and thirteen thousand were carried out over the course of eleven weeks; all burned beyond recognition. The troops were buried in a hush military ceremony in a place called Virginia, the infants put up for adoption on military bases. Butcher's followers were interred in various paupers' cemeteries around the country. It was all highly classified.

"The government was hard-pressed for an out, and

admission to genocide was definitely not an option. Solo. The Messiah Commission. Still Motion."

Seated at a broad table against the skin's southern face were seventeen dour men in age breaks measuring middle-aged to quite elderly. At first blush they presented all the appearance of colleagues posing for a group portrait, but closer examination exposed a panel of fuming arbiters going out of their way to avoid one another.

"Take a hard look at these very exclusive gentlemen. The commissioners were assigned to find a single, unassailable solution that would mollify the public, exonerate the government, and permanently prevent a recurrence of disaster on this scale. Finally admitting defeat, they narrowly passed a vote to solicit the assistance of a logic program. All pertinent data were entered. The program was unable to process the illogic of faith, but it established the *condition* of faith as the lynchpin, and demonstrated that this condition's insane consequences were made inevitable by an ages-old mindset under the mounting pressures of a burgeoning population. The Butcher explosion was cited as merely the initial catastrophe in a projected series of social cataclysms. The only-human commissioners were forced to beg the program for a livable solution, and the program responded in the time it takes to point a cursor:

"With Biblical references already deleted from record, with Butcher and his Tsunami followers all carbonized, and with the only people still shouting hosanna quarantined under military guard, the logical step was to delete those quarantined, establish means to obviate further religious influence from outside our borders, and rewrite history—a better history; one without smiting and persecution, one teeming with sane, dispassionate heroes. Something more palatable to subsequent generations. When prodded, the Commission's new digital tutor even offered up an improved version of reality. It simply removed everything related to religiosity, and left the great works of science and exploration intact.

"Yet that removal amounted, cumulatively, to thousands of years. The program, considering the way historical events were chronologically patterned, invented alternate causes and concerns. Prominent contemporary novelists, dramatists, and artists were commissioned to fill in the gaps, and their completed new history is pretty much the one we've grown up accepting as factual.

"Since the Commission refused to accept the liquidation of Butcher's followers, the program recommended they remain quarantined. It thereupon invented a mysterious virological factor, what became known as the 'Messiah Plague,' to justify an enforced isolation, projecting that, should these 'carriers' be allowed to die out naturally, the condition of religiosity would die out with them. In the meantime, the 'well' public would be told that the 'ill' Colonists' religious declamations were the natural result of an insidious, but completely contained, brain fever. As stipulated by the program, the government would keep up the necessary propaganda—quashing rumors and caramelizing facts—for as long as it took. According to the culled probability curves, Butcher's divinity would, in time, go the way of all rabble-rousers.

"The vote was seventeen over naught for revision on these terms.

"Gentlemen, I've come to appreciate the Messiah Commission's members as genuine heroes. Their regard for the betterment of our species far outweighed their personal wants. And, even though suicide was officially condemned by their deity, they'd made a pact. With the votes tallied, all seventeen sucked cyanide in a black-draped war room made up as a house of worship.

"Of course, the dying-out of Butcher's followers didn't solve a thing. They'd passed their beliefs onto their children, and when the youngsters grew up they smuggled in new converts from the cities. The Colony developed on its own underground, sequestered and provisioned by the government while it kept up the incurable disease ruse. But it's a funny thing about time. The brain adjusts beautifully. After centuries of repetition fiction 'becomes' truth. Even today, men thought to be snatchers are shot in cold blood by perfectly sincere agents. Mothers still spook their children with stories about carriers under the bed. Drunken teenagers still sneak into the Colony with guns and razors, still tell stories about fights to the death with subterranean zombie armies. Even though the Messiah Plague was yesterday's news four hundred years ago.

"Yet, you know, in the end that damned program was right. Men have come to favor their intellects over their passions. Our children grow up fascinated by the real rather than the imaginary. There's room for both humor and beauty in the grand mosaic."

Abel pushed himself to his feet. "*But*, Titus—humor and beauty aside, intellectual honesty prevents my accepting this notion of citizens wreaking havoc on their own civilization. Show me a war, show me a campaign—show me any time in history where so many people have behaved so violently in concert."

"You've got to absorb the psychological impact of this Bible-expunging thing, AJ. Imagine, as a comparison, all science wiped out, without the least vestige of evidence to show for centuries of heroic research."

"New calculations could be made. New heroes would arise."

Mack nodded, more to himself than to the room. "Well, there was one thing the Commission hadn't counted on, one thing the program wasn't able to deal with, one thing even Samuel Butcher wasn't ready for. As a matter of fact, millions upon millions of vigilant men and women were caught completely off guard."

"Of course they were." Abel's teeth glinted under the house lights. "And that would have been...*because?*"

"Do you remember that vision I mentioned earlier, the one that precipitated Sam's abrupt elevation to Messiah-hood? Solo. Vision One. Real Time. Full Pan, Short Zoom. Observer's Vantage, two-second delay."

And they were back outdoors on a black, searchlight-shredded night, locked elbow-to-elbow in a mob that stretched as far as the skin could capture. Now an incredible din—some kind of singsong chant—was cut off mid-verse. The projections surrounding the Group jerked to the northwest, their eyes bugged-out and their jaws hanging. As though choreographed, men and women on all sides immediately and simultaneously fell to their knees. The effect went out in the motion of ripples. Within seconds, projections horizon-to-horizon were flat on their bellies, facing a skull-shaped hill two hundred apparent-yards to the Group's left. In a hastily-cleared space atop that hill leaned a watery, free-standing shape. The figure was indisputably that of a man, as opposed to something manlike; the limbs were of human proportions and the bearing upright, though the spread arms and limp digits gave it an impression more of hanging than standing. Knees were closed, the pelvis sunken, the chin resting on the chest at a bad angle. It was a posture of complete submission to suffering, of spirit crushed, of life run out. In the area of the head could be seen spikes corresponding to rigid tufts, or perhaps to brambles or shards. The only indication of clothing was a series of lateral planes suggesting a rude cloth around the region of the loins. The phantom glowed dully in the night, so unstable it looked like it would phase out at any moment. Two seconds later it was hit by a hundred searchlight beams.

"Solo. Stop." Standing knee-deep in groveling humanity, Mack turned to Abel and said, "*Because*, Josh, it sure as hell looks like old Sam delivered."

Chapter Seven

Visions

Mack swept his arm at the hilltop phantom, stepping through bodies as he turned back.

"The anomaly came up pretty much by accident. I was monitoring what looked like a night rally, watching Sam scream himself hoarse on his big old sound stage. For all his frailty and advanced age, the man was an absolutely spellbinding orator. Fully swallowed up in bleating humanity, and still able to make himself heard. Phenomenal.

"That object appeared just as he was peaking. I say 'object' because I don't know what else to call it—it doesn't read normally. Every time Solomon puts out a seek, it pops up somewhere else around the planet, without any conformity to time or space; at least not as I understand them. We've followed it down through the ages, and seen awesome things: vintage warfare, natural calamities, odd movements of man and machine. More than that. To the bowels of prehistory, to the Cretaceous Age. Deeper. We've been all the way to the solar system's formation, just piggy-backing along with this thing. Solo. Resume."

The apparition seemed to flicker in the searchlights' beams. A second later it was gone. After a goose-pimpling minute of dead silence, the entire human panorama rose as though from sleep, threw out their million arms, and shrieked with boundless elation.

"Solo. Stop." The sound cut off cleanly.

"Soon after, the audio again becomes decipherable. The

72

crowd repeatedly chants the name 'Jesus,' as though soliciting the object's return."

"A contemporary of theirs?" Amantu wondered. "A celebrity, perhaps?"

"No, 'Jesus' was one of those 'sacrosanct' names, forbidden from casual usage during Butcher's era and, thanks to the Messiah Commission, buried since. I've had Solomon cross-reference it extensively, and all reads inevitably lead back to that humble little spot of sheep and shepherds. Solo. World Map Overlay. But lose the grid."

The floor disappeared; a room-sized scoop of foundation had just been replaced by apparent space. The skin now appeared backlit and papered blue, with the browns and greens of continents plainly delineated.

"The inverse image we're observing represents the world of two and a half centuries ago. Solo. Show us 'Galilee'." The great blue area was sucked aside, leaving a mostly-brown skin. "Jesus lived and died on this patch. He was born of a poor carpenter, and grew up to be one himself. It was a very harsh world back then, more like the Outs than our present, civilized society. Solo. Jordan, Real Time."

A dry plain surrounded by rolling hills under a hanging sun. Half a mile into the phantom horizon, a line of colorfully-robed men led a lazy line of dromedaries across an aching brown desert.

"As an adult, Jesus preached a kind of democratic doctrine that didn't sit at all well with authorities. Branded a fomenter, he was arrested, tried, and executed like a common thief just outside the city walls of a place called Jerusalem. Solo. The Crucifixion of Jesus. Zoom Out, Small Wide."

Four unseen figures on a ragged hillside, the Group cringed while a man wearing only a loincloth and a crown of thorns was nailed to a standing wood cross. His knot of kneeling observers cried out at each new agony, as though taking the blows themselves. Two other men, one on either side, already hung dead or dying. It was a wretched little scene, terribly painful to witness. Only the fact of its apparentness made it at all bearable.

"Solo. The Death of Jesus." Solomon reconfigured the

angle of sun, reducing the highlights and extending the shadows. The man on the center cross raised his eyes one last time, spoke a few words and dropped his head. As his body sagged the house lights came back up.

"That executed fellow," Amantu muttered. "Uncannily similar to the figure we observed only minutes ago. Your anomaly—the ghostly thing outside the caves."

Mack's eyes gleamed. "Solo. Vision One. Still Motion. Zoom in tight."

Night returned under the dome. Thousands upon thousands of prostrate followers were revealed, quadrant by quadrant, as Solomon ordered dense fields of data. The men now stood in that cleared space not two feet from the apparition; a very blurry, life-sized figure of a slumping man with arms raised to the sides and closed knees bent to his right. It was without doubt the crucified prisoner, straight down to the hints of a loincloth and brambly tiara, yet without any sign of a supporting cross. The same hard angle to the fallen chin, the same points of light marking forehead, cheekbone, and nose. There the sternum and ribcage, there and there the kneecaps and outer thighs. Mack and Amantu circled the specter from opposing poles, pondering details. The professor stopped and looked over a misty raised shoulder, directly into Mack's eyes.

"I am at a loss."

"Solo. Analyze." Mack bowed his head and looked back up. "What we're studying is unrelated to wavecluster images. This object represents a displacement of waveprints. There's nothing there."

"Yet now," Amantu observed coolly, "our nothing has a name. Solo. Cross-reference this projection with the person 'Jesus of Galilee'."

The skin became a fuzzy curved screen. Innumerable files were partitioned into a hemispherical grid, with each cell instantaneously producing its own sub-grid, and so on.

"Solo," said Mack. "Stop." The process froze startlingly, leaving the skin with a radiant byte-on-white wallpaper. This hard shift produced a strange subliminal effect akin to surfacing from a petit mal, complete with the necessary few seconds' mental recovery.

"Now there's some history for you, Professor. All these files pertain not only to the personage of Jesus, but to every contiguous datum, including affected persons, parties, and whole populations."

Amantu pulled himself out of it, his voice thick, his tongue a half-step behind his mind. "Then you have done this before."

"Over and over. Extensively. Habitually."

The room was absolutely silent. "Why, sir, am I here?"

"To observe. As a scholar and friend. Solo. Resume. Random Thumbnail, Fast Motion." Maybe a minute's worth of A/V graphics blew stuttering through the room, jumping centuries, climes, and participants. Women knelt, armies clashed, preachers raved. A dozen cities burned on the skin before Amantu, his brain reeling, barked,

"Solo! Stop!" The Group were in a stone hall somewhere, pondering a number of robed men poised like mannequins. Crude furniture, cheap utensils, simple décor; these were aesthetes. One man was frozen in the act of washing another's feet. Activity had been captured between steps, so that a ghostly transparency pervaded all. The stilted shafts of sun appeared more real than the projected solids.

Abel's eyes burned in the half-light. "Why show us all this carrier rot, Ti? As I see it, you're defeating your whole point here. These images would indicate an entire race of lunatics—spouting, flailing, and coalescing from Day One. Neither you nor your contraption will ever convince me that homo sapiens was mentally ill until four hundred years ago, when some mindless logic program set us straight."

"I'm not implying illness, AJ. We come from healthy stock."

"You think insanity's healthy?"

"These are the projections of men perfectly sane."

Abel and Izzy exchanged glances. The little psycho-analyst's jaw was hanging. Now his eyes relit and a slow smirk crept up his face. "Quite."

Mack tried Amantu directly. "We all know Solomon has the answers. Never in the history of thinking man has there been a real opportunity to put to rest the biggest question of all. As our resident historian, I think you should have the honor. What do you say, Professor? Would you like to see what all the brouhaha was about? Go ahead and judge for yourself. Just ask."

Amantu's head rolled up. There was something peculiarly comforting about the moment. His old programming was dissolving; he could feel it. For the first time in his life he understood the warmth of friendship; not as an annoying entertainment of the masses, but as a shared real-time experience, profound, whimsical, pregnant with memory-becoming. It struck him as a funny and very human thing to do; to accept the implied silly dare and step up to the plate. When he went into his old erect-with-hands-clasped stance this time, he did so with a boyish twinkle in his eyes. Amantu looked into his friends' expectant faces and said,

"All right, colleagues o'mine. I will bite." He grinned sarcastically. "Solo. Show me 'God'."

And the monks dissolved, and the skin went white. The moment froze. The world blew in.

And there was light.

Chapter Eight

The Honeycomb

Mack, realizing what had happened, was first to turn.

The Group's three-man reception committee stood shoulder-to-shoulder in the skin's breached north face, backed by the wide-open Outs. A filthy rag of a bandage peeked from beneath Micah's listing hood. "Did I lie?" he crowed, brandishing Abel's signet gleefully. "She goes 'Blinkety-blank, blinkety-blank. Bring us hither, lead us yon.' And so out of the wild we wanders, and into the Citydel we goes."

"He keyed me!" Abel spat. "The son of a bitch keyed me!"

Mack clenched his fists and snarled, "You *idiots!*" He took a huge breath. "Now wait just a minute. You people have no quarrel with us. There's a bunch of stuff in the bed and lab." He called back the Messrs Ivory. "This table alone is worth your trouble. Plus, there's food in the galley, and all the spirits you can handle. Just take what you want and go."

Micah's jaw dropped. "No quarrel?" He lifted the table with his peeling boot and kicked it sailing across the room. "I'll give you a quarrel, Barberus! This is all pilfered crap anyway. You'll pay, and pay sweet, for the trouble what you caused." He stepped up nose-to-nose with Mack while his mates moved laterally to cover the Group. "The same hilltop. The same first name, the same gang of googly-eyed gapers. But what gived you the right to flit off pretty whilst the good Lord suffered? That's what's got me ear up. Could it be you done a rat on him?" He whirled and stuck a finger in Izzy's face. "You'll get yours that much more for singing to the Pilot!" He turned back, said, "I salute ye!" and punched Mack flush in the nose. Before the astronomer could recover, Micah followed up with a left-right to the solar plexus. Mack went straight down. Micah repeatedly kicked him in the head while Ezekiel restrained Abel and Amantu by the throats. "You dirty thieving Barberus! You think you can run around jabbing forks in the tongues of serpents and the Good Lord'll just look the other way! Palms fifty-two double-dot thirteen: 'This is *my* bloody bread, Yahoo!' Well, you old spiller of fire, Mama's got a special space reserved just for you!" He hauled Mack up by the hair, slammed his back against the skin and spat in his glassy eyes. "Chris!" he shouted, slapping him hard across the right cheek. "Cross!" and he back-slapped the left cheek. *"Double-cross!"* He slapped him back and forth, then whipped out his blade. "North!" He slashed Mack's forehead. "East!" He stabbed him in the right palm. "West!" He stabbed the other hand and hurled the blade upright in the floor. "South, you bastard!" He kneed him directly in the scrotum. Mack was unconscious before he hit the floor.

"Enough!" Abel cried. "You'll kill him!"

Micah turned slowly, his hood tilting side to side. "Haven't we—didn't we—ain't we spake before? I could of sweared—" His eyes lit up in their painted splotches. "Blinkety-blank! Blinkety-blank!" Up went Micah's great sledge of a fist. Down it came on Abel's waiting crown. The big man snatched Malachi's noose and lash, drew the rope tight around the necks of Amantu, Abel, and Izzy, and snapped the whip twice before handing it back. "Hippity-hop, me lambs! Mal, you'll be escorting our three fairy friends, and Easy, you'll be helping me along with our little cross-jumper here." Ezekiel obediently took one of Mack's arms. Micah squeezed under the other, and they hauled him out like a load of dirty laundry. Malachi, shrieking and lashing all the while, dragged and goaded the Group along behind. Ezekiel's and Micah's eyes flashed every time they checked back over their shoulders. Micah abruptly wheeled under Mack's dangling arm and began to backpedal. Proceeding thusly, with Ezekiel still pacing directly and Mack's toes

passively plowing the filth, he commenced a running mono-
logue.

"We ain't real partial to city slime. Y'*hear* me? That's a
naughty little mess you made in the hole, and it won't be us
what'll be cleaning her up. And that big white light what you
shot—we gots laws about bringing fancified technology downstairs. That's just one more count against you; one of many. Let
me read 'em to you straight, just in case you feel you ain't
getting the good Lord's justice. Le's see now. They's moral
trespass, burnt offings, and cavern images, not to mention
wearing clashing blouses and tippy-toeing through the Outs in
the first place. But most of all you been conspiring with a thief.
Don't think we ain't been watching you prissy pirates over the
years, and don't think we just done met all accidental-like back
there. You gots careless; you gots caught. Should of stuck to the
well-beat path, like always. We had our eyes on Barbs here for
the longest time; he's 'Number Three for the Cavalry,' as we
likes to call him. A big gun, indeed." He did a goofy pirouette,
forcing Ezekiel to turn along with Mack between them. The
doctor's arms were now strung out in a mockery of crucifixion.
"Ain't she pretty?" Micah beamed. "Just how she's gonna look
for Mama." He studied Mack critically before raising the
drooping head with a fist, singing, "Look up, little thief, look up
for a while! Show us that long-long 'waited, dead man's smile."
Mack's head rolled off the fist. Micah frowned. "No sleeping on
the set!" He began slapping Mack's slack face back and forth.

Ezekiel laughed and drew back his free arm. He was just
balling up his fist when Abel, barely cognizant, bleated, *"Animals!"*

Micah and Ezekiel froze as though electrocuted. They
ratcheted round to stare, their painted jaws hanging. Micah
stepped from under the arm and Mack dropped in a heap.

It was a break. The men squirmed free of the noose and
lunged forward while Malachi hung back snapping the whip and
looking stupid. Hurriedly lifting Mack upright, the reformed
Group created a tight shield of interlaced arms.

"Security!" Micah howled. "The prisoners is revolting!"

Ezekiel called back, "Is they ever!"

All three brigands leaped on the living shield, laughing,

peeling away fingers and wrestling back arms. The surrounded Group scrapped hysterically, and for a crazy few seconds it appeared the hooligans might actually be beaten back.

Out of the confusion came a chunk of metal debris, hard onto Abel's tender skull. Everything stopped on a dime. In a few seconds the action resumed centripetally, but it was hard to tell who was doing the pushing and who the pushing-back, for the men were all tied up around the two principals like Sumo wrestlers. Abel lay on the verge of unconsciousness, peering up at a raving Ezekiel. It was a situation right out of every school-boy's nightmare—the restrained onlookers, the looming bully planted squarely over your midsection with his legs spread wide and his fists clenched. Abel dribbled something incoherent.

Ezekiel hauled him up by the collar.

"*What* did you call me, punk?" He cocked back an arm and threw a haymaker that almost broke Abel's jaw. Ezekiel then dropped to his knees, directly onto Abel's passively splayed forearms, and began whaling with both fists about the skull and face. "*What* did you call my mama? *Huh*, queerboy?"

If not for Malachi, Ezekiel might have beaten Abel to death right then and there. At a barked command from Micah he used his whip to drag Ezekiel off by the throat, then swung him round to face the leader, who merely slapped his lieutenant back and forth and was done with it. The big man easily righted Abel and dusted him off. He checked the tongue, rolled back an eye-lid. "How you feeling, son?" Abel jerked away his head. Micah fluffed up his hair and wagged a big gloved finger in his face. "Now don't you think you owe Easy here a 'pology? What you said wasn't real nice at all." Abel lowered his eyes.

"He's sorry, sir," Izzy called. "Really he is."

Micah turned and pensively considered the shivering doctor. After a long minute he breathed, "I should certainly hope so," and bent to lift Mack. Then, with Micah gloomily dis-coursing on the paucity of city manners, the party inched across the Outs, much subdued. But the nearer they came to that filthy hole, the lighter his temper grew, and by the time they'd reached the camouflaged entrance he was all genial host.

"Welcome one, welcome all! The whole crowd's a-waiting. They's snacks in the rats' nests and blood in the gutters. Now you get your blasphemous butts down them steps, and don't pleat your petticoats in the process."

But the captives were so shaky, and their captors so heavy-handed, that the whole human knot went tumbling head over heels. At the bottom there was a blind grope-and-scuffle, and when the Group were finally raised by the scruffs of their necks the brigands were thoroughly pissed. Micah shook them one by one, like dusty rugs. "Now don't you be in such a hurry to get to the party! And once you're mingled you best not bother trying to run." He jerked a thumb at the bright chamber. "You in your silky dandies—with all that floundering flesh in there you'll stick out like flags." Following through on his own gesture, he stomped up to the opening and, in a stance reminiscent of the Group's first entrance, leaned in with his hands braced on the walls and yelled, "Hosea! Nahum! Let go of that sphincter and get over here. We gone and bagged us the big one!" Two similarly costumed brutes pushed their way in, leering at the Group. Their painted-round eyes lit up at the sight of Mack. Roughly hoisting him between them, they swung back into the light and began lashing out with their tatterdemalion boots. Micah smacked his big hands together. "Okay! Mal, get the gate. Easy, hold this harlot still so's I can brand her." A familiar scrape and rattle, and the gate came crashing down. Izzy almost jumped out of his socks at the sound. Dead sober, he leapt for the side tunnel with Abel hard on his heels.

Micah snatched their collars. "Not this time you don't! And none of your slickety-tricks, neither." He tossed his head. "Boys!" Malachi and Ezekiel immediately commenced a very physical, very comprehensive, and very humiliating search of the prisoners. They weren't in the least shy; this was a head-to-foot, full-body cavity examination. By the time they were done, the Group were meek as lambs. "You're *going* to see the Possle," the big man proclaimed, "so just you clippety-clop along there!"

"What's a—" Abel whined, pulling up his shorts, "—for Christ's sake, sir, what's a *postle*?"

"The Possle's our wise man. He's a thinker and a stinker and a real pretty boy. And he's the one who's gonna spit on your phony story before Mama gores you. Used to be twelve, according to the Black Book, but a certain little *Judas*," and he kicked Izzy squarely in the behind, "poisoned all their suppers. Now *move*, the lot of you!"

The cavern was hot from the heads of a hundred leaping torches. Everywhere were naked, soot-smeared men and women, many of them cripples, pulling themselves along the rock floor and into black recesses, their moans tinged with the strangest inflection of rapture. At the sight of prisoners being kicked through the chamber, these unfortunates began screaming insanely, slapping legs and faces, biting themselves and anyone proximate. The Group, calling out to one another in the most plaintive fashion, were shoved hopping and squealing through the flopping shiny bodies. Micah squeezed between them, shouting into their ears.

"So you think this is exciting, do you? You should see it when the new queen gets mated, man! I already been privy to twice of them juicy little affairs in me lifetime. The whole place turns into a great big nonstop orgy; blood and guts *everywhere!* And the lucky stiff what gets to pitch the goods, man—well, he's just like torn *to bits* by the crowd. Literally, baby! Smashety-smite! Bashety-boom! And so off to God he goes, whilst the queen hunkers back down to her flogging."

"You mean—" Amantu gasped, "you mean to say you *torture* your leader?"

"From the day she's old enough to sing in the key of pain! She's *cultivated*, man. Bred to take it and love it, bred to show 'em all how Jesus took it and loved it. That's the ticket, me little fickle-footed Judas goats: the key to immortality is takin' it! All you gots to do is peek into the Black Book, though I personally doubts your gentlemen's pee would have the stuff to render a decent read. God loves to see us suffer. Loves it! Just take a look at the world. And, since God do duly love him what suffers for Him, it only stands to reason He loves him most what suffers for Him most."

"But no culture—" Izzy gasped "—no culture can subsist on pain! Mercy and compassion are what bond us. Your leaders must be sensitive to grief. Your women must yield to their tender nature. For Christ's sake, man, *everybody* can't be inured to pain!"

Micah punched him thoughtfully. "Oh, they's a whole spectrum of sorts what lives down here. Some manages from the shadows, some snatches city folk, some works for real like me and the boys, and some wallows in mindless bliss like these swimming pretty parasites. Now us, we's what's knowed as butchers. We keeps the floor babies in line with a stomp and a bite and a good Godly gonading, but, y'see, the real reason these crawly goobers is so into it is cause they's soft. Soft in the psyche. Their relations schools 'em in the ways of God, and they just goes bonkos with the whole process. They's a long rite of passage—who can lay out the most slapping around, then who can take it best, then who can deal it to his self with the hardest eye, and so on. I mean, after generations like." He looked around disdainfully. "Sure as David stoned the Big Guy, no regular man started out goosing his self. I mean," he said diplomatically, "they do very truly believes in the One Holy— as does we all—but they gots it *bad*, man. They gots the Bug."

"One point," Abel tried, "*sir*—just a word about that postulated pestilence. We've only recently witnessed recorded evidence regarding a massive governmental cover-u—"

"Flog all that!" Micah twisted Abel's and Izzy's collars in his fists, then hammered their heads forward and backward rapidly, like a man doing an intensive workout set. "One word about that postulated government, Senators! Y'all been playing screw-me since the day before anyone can remember who first begetted who and whatever became of whatnot! But what we *do* know is that your super-great-great granddaddies done something really Lucyfur-dark a long-long time ago, okay?"

"Four hundred yea—" Amantu got out before taking Ezekiel's elbow in the ribs.

Micah turned his fright-face on the professor. "*I don't give a good holy-arse damn* about what all your little-dots machines says! You got me? I spits on your unholy works and lies. It's *you* what gots us down here in the first place! But, that spat, I'm yet to see a truly sick man in these here caves. The folks is just nuts cause they's programmed. And, like I said, cause they's soft. Still—and I'll be thumbing out your ugly city eyes at the moment you scumsuckers sees it—we gots *God*, and that's something you damned atheists'll *never* get back!"

"Exactly!" snipped Abel. "No plague! Official lie—terrible thing—most egregious nature! But sir, *please*, the whole divinity business...our friend Titus discovered an anomaly—it's—it's—how do I put it—"

"It's a lie is what it is! Everything what comes from machines and thinking mens is lies, meant only to cast dirty thought-clouds on he what climbed up on the cross and taked it for us! You remember that when you're begging the Possle to keep your innies, you nasty agnostics. And I want you to go ahead and tell him it was Micah who gived you the pew on it all." He grabbed a fistful of Izzy's butt and squeezed until the psychoanalyst screamed. "And tell him I said 'go easy' on the little one."

Malachi and Ezekiel were delighted by Izzy's cry of pain. Malachi shrieked and flapped in circles, while Ezekiel howled, "Whoo-oo! I says *whoo-oo-oo!"*

"S-s-s-city," Malachi hissed, "for s-s-s-sinn—"

"Tis a fact," Micah said, nodding gravely. "Down here the Lord don't take no prisoners. And he don't like conspirators none, neither. Separate, you three is just warts and bunions. Together, you gots what's knowed as sin-ergy."

"But it's all madness!" Izzy wept. "It's madness, madness! It's madness, pure and plain!"

"*Mad*, are we? What of you, up in your ugly ivy towers with all your filthy phony finery? You think God loves you for your pretty buttons and badges? All you rich men, sticking your stinking silver needles into the eyes of camels!" He spat directly in Izzy's face. "You bastards! I never even *seen* a camel!"

With his elbows pressed against his ribs, Izzy could only flap his little tyrannosaur hands and cry, "Me neither! But you fellows have us all wrong! We're professional men; not capitalists, not epicureans. And we certainly aren't affiliated with any governmental agencies!"

"Oh, yeah? What do you do for a living?"

"I'm a psychoanalyst, sir."

"And her?"

"Professor Amantu's an historian working day and night to understand those atrocities responsible for your unwarranted situation down here, that they may be rectified for the betterment of all. Titus Mack, the man you keep calling Barbara, is also involved in work to save the Colony."

"And your bigmouthed girlfriend?"

"Abel Lee is an ex-medical practitioner and legal mediator. Nowadays he speaks at universities and councils. He can direct your grievances to the proper offices. We can *all* help you! We're not the bad guys here. We're your friends!"

"Saints! And all this time we thoughts you was sent by Beezly Bub his self! How could we of been so wrong? You only *looks* like a Roman, Senator!" He took Izzy by the hair and whirled him round twice before hurling him feet-first into the sea of naked groping humanity. "Professional men, eh? Well, Mister Ain't-Affiliated—psychoanalyze them!" Undaunted by Amantu's bulk, he tore the professor out of Ezekiel's headlock and repeated the process. "Rectify *that*, you old Black Prince, you!" Lastly went Abel. "Mediate away, Philistine!" The man seemed even bigger and more vital for all his expended energy. He ripped the bandage from his head, raised his fists lustily, and roared like a gorilla. While his cohorts picked out distracted specimens to slap, he went wading through the glistening arms and legs, occasionally reaching down for a tongue to yank or an eye to gouge. "Brethren! Who amongst ye covets the services of *professional* men? Come to them for courteous counsel, seek their hands for pain over pity. What's that? You have no gold to jangle? You fear they will do their precious punishing elsewhere? Well, *we*, me lambs, are not so mercenary! We dole it out for free!" He kicked a man in the mouth and received a gargling scream of pleasure.

Momentarily forgotten, the Group pawed through the thrashing mass until their foreheads met. They peeked from behind a hot mound of lolling limbs. Their sadistic guards were looking this way and that, moving away gradually while stomping and punching. With their ominous peaked shadows reeling against the spit-and-hiss of torches, the brutes appeared colossal and unreal.

"Disrobe immediately!" Abel gasped.

Amantu gasped right back, *"Sir!"*

"It's the only way, Hammer. Remember what he said about us standing out like flags? Well, he's right. We've got to

85

blend in." He shoved a sooty arm from his face. "This is no time for modesty. I don't like the sound of this postle-person."

Izzy went absolutely white. "I'll *not!* We're educated men. We have shame, we have refinement. Dignity's all that separates us from this mob."

"These robes," Amantu mumbled, "have great significance."

"Then give my regards to the postle. Look, we don't have to discard our clothes, just screen them. Keep 'em bundled out of sight."

"Reprobates?" called Micah, some thirty feet away. The Group dug deeper. Following Abel's lead, Izzy and Amantu wriggled out of their robes and slithered through the bodies like worms, becoming increasingly moist and smudged. Abel led them to the nearest wall, and there elbowed out a channel along the jutting rock.

"Ugh," Izzy grunted, pushing off a woman either dead or unconscious.

"Shut up!"

"Sybarites?"

The men moved along the wall as one long segmented creature; crowns to soles, right hands clutching tightly rolled clothing, left hands brushing aside hair and assorted appendages. The occasional scarred face popped in raving.

Abel urged them into a side-chamber with fewer torches and occupants, assuming, from then on, lead-man position. One wall of the chamber was a massive stone oven. There were crude ceramic plates on cut-rock tiers. The place reeked of burnt fat.

It was all very close. Firelight played on the shadows, protrusions leapt and shrank. The nude Group members held their clothes uncomfortably, while Izzy turned a radiant crimson. They were just getting decent when Amantu, over-cautious with his robes, dropped the whole mess and left himself, for one agonizing moment, frontally, fatally, and fully exposed. Every eye was drawn to the spot.

"Hammer!" Abel managed, as Amantu's hands raced to cover his heart. "I didn't—I don't—I—"

"Aortic surgery," the Professor admitted. "A shunt was

customized."

"Atheists!"

Izzy blushed even deeper. "I humbly apologize, Hammer, for having goaded you earlier. Had I known—"

"Oh, *posh*," Amantu mumbled, "'Izzy.'"

"Gone! They's in the Honeycomb!"

"Run like hell," Abel cried. They threw themselves into their robes and ran, not caring who or what they stepped on. The natural order of flight held sway: lanky Abel, corpulent little Izzy, and finally the thickset, puffing professor. The men ducked into a high, tube-like tunnel, letting Abel make the spot decisions whenever they came upon forks. It wasn't long before they'd completely lost their thudding predators. Mounted torches grew rarer and weaker; on certain long sections of wall they'd petered out altogether. Faced with an endless choice of side-tunnels, some blind, some leading into tapering, pitted blowholes, Abel tentatively led them down a particularly dark left-hand passage into a surprisingly well-lit tunnel. Catching the sounds of stomping and shouting, they took a number of kneejerk zigs and zags, finally huddling in the dark against a warm left-hand wall.

"Halls," Izzy panted. "Natural. Tunnels bored out." He blinked at the rock. "Maybe only—maybe just scraped out."

Abel whispered, *"Duck!"* The men scrabbled into niches. After half a minute's dead silence they heard hard running, advancing in one breath and receding the next.

Izzy peeked from his hole, said, "The acoustics are odd," and immediately retracted his head like a turtle. "I thought—" His eyes rolled to the tunnel's ceiling. Clopping noises met overhead and radiated in all directions. "But...balls descending!"

The Group crept out of hiding and snuck between torches by touch, hitting the floor every time the clattering was repeated.

"They've got to be just as confused," Abel said, peeking into a passage with a zillion capillaries. "What did the big one call this place?"

"The Honeycomb," Amantu mumbled. "The selfsame term related by Doctor Mack—by Titus, that is." He visually measured apparent blind alleys in the roof and walls. "And Doctor Weaver is correct. The earth has been worked extensively, perhaps over decades. Yet—there is a peculiar unfinished quality to the narrower passages. Do you men see these grooves? What instrument would produce them?"

Abel's fingers inspected a series of scored marks. "At all costs we must find Ti."

"Sound guidance. Lead on, 'AJ'."

Abel crept side-to-side and rarely looked back, checking torches and tunnel floors like a mountain lion studying branches and prints. This Honeycomb section was riddled with narrowing tunnels and partial excavations, with cells and burrows, with stairways to empty pits, with chipped-out handholds to no-where. Some passageways were lit, some bare, but nearly all contained branches, wells, and flues. One of the brighter tunnels revealed warrens housing mangled bodies in varying degrees of decomposition. Abel availed himself of a sputtering torch with one hand, cupped the other over his mouth and nose, and stepped tenderly through the well-rounded portals. Outside a particularly large chamber, an enormous cross had been gouged out of the facing tunnel wall. This place featured a vault containing—along with the ubiquitous pocks, holes, and fissures— ranks of vertically aligned berths holding the skeletons of people hanged, pummeled, and otherwise murdered.

Izzy winced over Abel's shoulder. "Ugh. Criminals, you think?"

"I'm not sure. There's a message chipped out of the rock under this berth. It says, 'Daniel, 2:29'. And under that it reads, *'Think in thy bed'*." He straightened. "Not a whole lot to think about, now, is there?"

"Mine's name was Joel," Izzy mumbled. "And he was 2:23, whatever that means. It says here, *'Be joyful'*."

"Well, he certainly does seem to be smiling." Abel moved down the line. "Here's a guy named Amos. Amos, 7:12. Amos has an admonition. It says, *'Go, flee away'*."

"Sage advice."

"These bones," mused the professor, "appear to have been gnawed." He peered deeper into the berths. "The cradles open into pitch. Can these be the mouths of burrows?"

"Then it's true!" Izzy cried. "The rumors!" His whole frame crimped. *"Cannibals!"*

"Shh!"

Crunching gravel, clipped exchanges. It was too late to flee, and too late to kill the torch. The men could only squeeze into a crouching huddle.

The jagged shadows of Malachi and Ezekiel rippled along the tunnel wall like animated cave paintings. Hard running at the other end quickly diminished to padding, and a moment later Micah's shadow was leaning in to join the others. For the longest time the trio of shadows vacillated there, without budging. Finally Micah's voice bounced round the tunnel. "You know that smell what living folk gives off when they's around the dead?"

"I stink I do," Ezekiel replied.

"Comes from horror. Their gonads hitch up and the funk wells out of every pore. Only one smell's got a sweeter stink than horror."

"And what stink would that be?"

"Terror," Micah said. "Makes a man a veritable cold-sweat flower. And when they's more'n one around, that big ol' stink makes for a downright dandified bouquet."

Ezekiel leaped in to one side, his eyes gleaming from Abel's trembling torch. "Chris!" he cried and, pinching his nose, appended, "Pee-ee-*you!"*

Malachi, hopping in on the other side, yelled, "C-c-cross!" and stood grinning with his fists on his hips, a psychotic adult Peter Pan.

The warren's opening was now a hellish mantelpiece; Malachi and Ezekiel the side-lit ogre bookends, fully-illuminated Micah the oval-framed grinning portrait. Micah, stepping aside to expose the gouged-out cross, said pleasantly, "And Double-Cross! It taked some fancy slitherings, but you three serpents appears to have done-finded the perfect hole."

Ezekiel and Malachi began a creepy flanking maneuver; darting their heads like snakes while flicking their tongues and flapping their arms. The Group instinctively bunched into a line, pushing Abel forward. He waved his torch back and forth uncertainly, holding it on Malachi after a faked attack. "Wawa," said Malachi. "Wawa, wawa." He grimaced and gritted. "Wa-wa-watch my eyes. Not my-ha, not my-ha, not my-ha."

He flapped his robe urgently, distracting Abel long e-nough for Ezekiel to take an enormous sideways stride. But Abel parried swiftly, shifting the torch one to the other. "I don't wish to hurt you, sirs."

Ezekiel shook his hood hard. "*Wrong!* Don't watch *me*. Watch *him*."

Upon this cue he rushed forward. Abel swung to meet him directly, allowing Malachi to swoop in from the side.

Amantu's black hand was the tip of a lash, plucking the torch from Abel's fist and jabbing it side-to-side like an epee: flame-first into Malachi's snarling mask, then, in the same twisting thrust, base-downward onto the closing crown of Eze-kiel. Both freaks hit the floor screaming. The action froze. Everybody dropped what they were doing and stared at the professor with a new respect.

Now, Moses Matthew Amantu was a most imposing man, physically as well as intellectually. With a spitting torch in his hand he was fearsome enough to give even a backward bully like Micah pause. Abel and Izzy clambered into berths, squeal-ing as they scrambled through rotted remains. They wiggled blindly down adjoining passages, pausing to call back plaintive-ly before wiggling on.

Micah and Amantu stared each other down in the pe-tering torchlight; a pair of facing stalagmites. The only sounds were the receding calls of Abel and Izzy, along with Malachi's hissing whimpers, and an occasional rolling moan from Ezekiel. In time even these prominent noises were swallowed up in the Honeycomb. Still that stare went on. The torch coughed and sighed; light left the chamber as though a dimmer switch were being adjusted by an unseen hand. And still that stare went on. Now darkness permeated the warren's interior, broken only by the intense afterglow of two steady pairs of locked eyes.

Without looking away, Amantu quietly set down the spent torch, adjusted his robes, and slipped into the hewn-away berth.

His friends were still calling back when he came up to them on his hands and knees.

"Hammer!" Izzy gasped. "You are truly a man! We might have been—we could have been—we certainly *would* have been—"

"Prudence," observed the professor in the dark, "would dictate we press on."

"Hear, Hear!" coughed Abel. "Follow me." But he didn't budge. The men could hear him breathing hard. A minute later firelight was leaping behind them.

Izzy poked him in the rear. "Then *move*, damn you!" Spiders in a drainpipe, the Group slapped down their palms and scuttled on.

Chapter Nine

Caverns

T here was no shortage of forks or tributaries, no end to the side-tunnels, pits, and alcoves—yet not a single passage even once reached a height that would allow the men to ease their aching backs. While being pursued they were able to navigate visually, albeit with much knuckle-scraping and wounding of knees. But soon even the partial illumination of torchlight was replaced by the dreariest of ignes fatui.

"I'm *dying!*" Izzy cried, slamming cheek-to-cheek with Amantu. "I'm parched, I'm faded, I'm fagged!" He lolled on his back, licking his lifeless lips. "Anyways, they're not following us anymore. They've got to know something we don't."

"Like?"

"Like maybe all these little tunnels terminate in a mass cul-de-sac. You never stopped to consider that? Or like maybe they *do* have exits, but in places those maniacs know all about."

Amantu wiped his face. "It is imperative we develop a means of recognition beyond our posteriors. There is space e-nough to retire this most unbecoming single-file procession."

"A bad plan, man. We can't afford to separate—not in the dark, and certainly not for the sake of moral decorum."

"Yet we are blind, AJ, in object as well as in sight. What purpose do we serve in sneaking up on the unknown?"

"Hammer's right, Josh. Since we're not being followed, it makes a hell of a lot more sense to double back to the tunnels. Those madmen are probably swinging around ahead of us even as we speak."

"Then what're those lights behind us?"

"Spots before your eyes; they're still adjusting. It's residual illumination."

"I perceive them also. Yet many more than anticipated. Dozens, shining steadily, and from several angles." A scratch-and-patter in a passage to their right. A chorus of squeals to their rear. The Group froze exactly as they were; not breathing, not even blinking.

Being thinking men, they weren't particularly phobic about rodents. To the contrary, Abel was an avid squirrel-feeder, Izzy kept three golden hamsters as office pets, and Amantu had rescued a dozen black rats from university labs. But the creatures now gathering about them were a different breed altogether.

With grain, seed, and vermin in short supply, four centuries of subterranean adaptation had produced an outsized animal that fed almost exclusively on human remains. Fatting originally on discarded body parts, then, as competition grew, on entire cadavers, the Honeycomb Rat developed into an aggressive, almost fearless predator, averaging in size somewhere between a large pug and a small warthog. The characteristic squeals made visual identification unnecessary.

"Oh no!" wept Izzy. "Oh, *no*-no-no. Not like this."

"Don't be ridiculous!" Abel's voice rose an octave per syllable. "They can't be after *live* meat!"

"Shoo!" Amantu smacked down a palm. *"Scat!"* The squeals increased in intensity.

"Don't antagonize them!" Abel cried. "Everybody remain perfectly calm!" There was a hiss and clatter almost at his elbow. Abel scrambled away screaming, Izzy and Amantu close behind.

The rats made horrible snuffling sounds as they scurried. They slammed their fellows against walls, nipping one another in their passion. Those in the fore savaged competitors popping in from side tunnels, and when the victors came upon Amantu's furiously wagging behind there was no mistaking their intent. The lead rat bit into a flapping sandal and refused to let go, though the bellowing professor kicked frantically. Another leaped right over the leader, momentarily attaching itself to

Amantu's back before being scraped off by the tunnel's roof. Amantu thereupon veered into a broader side passage. He whipped off his sandals and slapped them madly. Those rodents just behind the original leaders then went after Izzy, who plunged into a left-hand gap, incidentally joining Amantu. The two ricocheted through this parallel tunnel, calling to Abel at apertures. But their lanky leader had completely lost his cool. His constant screaming produced a matching frenzy in the rats; they poured by like rank water, fighting for fang-holds.

"Josh!" Izzy called desperately, and flung himself into the squealing stream.

Rats *do not* like being approached from behind. When Izzy sprang in hollering they whirled and hissed menacingly, but, vile cowards that they are, made to scatter rather than re-taliate. Biting at anything and everything, the largest scraped along the walls, snapping wildly and trampling smaller members. Amantu hauled the psychoanalyst back in, but it was too late for their friend. Abel kicked and scraped along until he found himself upright, his head and shoulders protruding into a diagonally-running upper passage. He swung in on his belly while the rats rushed in below, leaping and gnashing.

Abel plunged down his head. "Professor!"

No answer.

"*Izzy!*"

Nothing but the sounds of squealing and snapping. He jerked back and pulled himself through the dark, relying on toes, elbows, and fingernails.

Before he'd managed a yard the rats were on him. But even as he turned screaming he was swallowed up in a sinkhole-like depression. With a dozen rats tumbling behind him, Abel slid headfirst down a rock chute into a huge calcite cavern, lit surreally by a bluish phosphorescent powder that clung to every limestone face. The last thing he remembered was a fissure plugged by waving snouts. Abel ran blindly, barking his shins and elbows, gasping: "Eaten alive. Eaten alive. Poor little Izzy. Eaten alive." When he was all run-out he stopped, pressed a hand to his side, and squinted into the drear.

The great cavern possessed a somber, cathedral-like quality; steep walls brushed longitudinally by that soft blue powder, along with occasional thick calcite streaks that lent an impression of gigantic painted windows. The silence was bottomless.

Abel stumbled up to a pool ringed by stalagmites. The pool contained a single fat, milky-white cave pearl, deposited drop by drop from a teat-shaped stalactite a centimeter above. Over time a corresponding stalagmite had developed from the pool's basin; this growth now rose from the pool like a lily's pistil. The cave pearl was floating in equipoise, at the precise center of dripping stalactite and rising stalagmite, patiently awaiting that one sweet finalizing drop. Between the cavern's floor and the pool's rim ran a bench-shaped outcropping smoothed by centuries of overflowing rainwater. The bench seat completely spanned the pool, at one point dipping out of view. It was a natural place to rest.

Abel flopped against the seat's elegantly bowed back, his elbows dipping into the murky pool. He angrily snatched up the pearl and hurled it ricocheting across the cavern. Echoes raced away like some large obscure animal, but the clatter was clearly preceded by a hard little yelp.

He hit the floor. "Who's there?"

"Ow-*ow!*"

"Malachi?" Abel backpedaled carefully. "Are you alone, man? I don't want any trouble with anybody."

It's true what they say about one's senses sharpening in the dark. Abel's ears picked up minute movements and sounds, and in half a minute he made out the triangular figure of Malachi crouching on a dusty outgrowth with his cloaked arms tucked in like wings. Malachi's Colony-eyes were well-adapted to subterranean predation. Perceiving Abel's shift in focus, he leapt silently and with accuracy onto a projection ten feet away. Immediately a fat swarm of bats, ghostly-white against the phosphor's soft blue, burst out of a crevice and took off screaming.

"Talk to me, Mal." Desperation crept into Abel's voice. "Let's work something out."

The craggy shape approached rock-by-rock. "God's gonna get—gonna get—God's getcha gonna—gonna getcha—"

Abel tripped over a low calcite spill and scooted away

blind. "This is not the time or place, Mal. We can rationalize. We can deal."

"G-God doesn't deal, say the Book. No-not with sin— not with sinn—"

"Not *now*, Mal! Look, I can get you stuff. Real stuff, not promises. Me and my friends are big shots in the city. We've got connections." Abel ducked into a narrow passage between ribbed outcroppings. "How long's it been since you had a good steak, with all the trimmings? How's about a nice Chianti?"

Malachi rose almost directly above him, cawed, "Sliver tongue!" and swept up his arms. "'P-prick and be done,' say the Book. 'It's meorma, meorma—it's me or Mama.'" One hand dipped under his cloak. Even in the dimness, the seven-inch blade showed cleanly. "'Poke the pi—p-poke the pig,' say the Book. 'Poke the pig to s-save the circle.'"

Abel screamed, wheeled, and bolted straight into a wall at the end of a cul-de-sac. He expected an answering shriek from Malachi, so he was amazed to hear his own name called out in response. The voice was unmistakable, and appeared to be coming right out of the wall.

"Izzy!"

"Here, Josh!"

"Professor!"

"And here!"

At another blast of flapping wings, Abel spun around with his arms covering his face. But the twisted spire of Malachi was gone. Abel turned back.

"You're alive!"

"Very much so. Although our circumstances would recommend an ellipsis be placed on that assertion. How are you situated?"

"I've got company. Malachi's in here somewhere, but he took off when he heard you guys calling."

"Do not alter your position! We are experiencing another of these caverns' acoustical phenomena."

"How's Izzy?"

A snarl appeared slightly to Abel's left. "Okay, Josh. But so help me, if I ever get out of here alive—"

"Damn it, Izzy! Hammer's right. This is a major break,

and we'll have to work in concert. All right?"

"Agreed."

"Whatever."

Abel placed his lips on the rock. "Don't change positions, don't raise or lower your heads, don't look away. Face my voice directly, both of you, and continue to speak in measured tones. Judging by its feel, this whole wall's riddled with grooves and recesses. I'll proceed gradually to my right while you guys match my pace to your left, until we either encounter one another or our voices grow distant. If the latter, we'll all just as carefully retrace our steps to this point and try again to our left. Sooner or later we'll meet, or at least find the aperture that's making it possible to communicate."

Amantu said, with exaggerated clarity, "I heartily approve of this plan, AJ. We are facing your voice now, and will endeavor to move with the utmost synchronicity. That said, we are prepared to proceed."

A minute passed. "Christ," Izzy muttered, "I'd trade my practice for a drink."

"Do not turn your face. You heard the man. Both parties must behave concordantly."

The head swiveled defiantly. Izzy could just discern the faint outline of Amantu's wooly skull. "How long must the blind lead the blind? Why'd you have to drag me along with you, anyway?"

Amantu very slowly turned his head until he was looking down at the psychoanalyst's dim naked crown.

"Charity too can be blind. I was prey to a rash impulse, in hindsight apparently unwarranted. Nevertheless, that quick reaction preserved your ample carcass from a horde of stampeding man-eaters."

"One rat over many. Josh! For Christ's sake, get me out of here!"

"There is no reply. There is nothing! We have lost our sole connection. Who knows how rare that phenomenon might be?"

"You're the one who 'guided' us here! 'Here' being a foot-wide ledge in utter darkness."

"*Must* you whine in perpetuity? I led us to our colleague,

did I not? This labyrinth, as we have observed, is peppered with means of egress. And the darkness is not utter; you exaggerate, as ever. That source of luminosity is nearer than I anticipated. *Do* press on, Doctor Weaver. You are blocking the road."

They argued back and forth along the precipice, feeling their way hand-over-hand until they'd stepped out upon an immense smooth-faced rock overlook. Below was a dank cavern full of massive stalagmites, petered-out stalactites, and the occasional glistening column. Illumination was provided by a pair of jagged apertures on the far wall. A single row of stalagmites rose out of the abyss like volcanic islands, forming a daunting bridge between that wall and the basaltic monolith now supporting Amantu and Izzy. To the bridge's right ran a wide curtain of cerebella-like calcite flows, and to its left was an impenetrable void. The professor sounded that void with a dropped pebble that pinged back and forth until it was swallowed by silence. "A bottomless basin," he noted. "A sinkhole for the ages. Our Honeycomb may be worked over by man, but she is eaten away by nature."

Izzy sat hard. "And so here we die." He slid a foot before braking with his palms. "The Mercies' flickering lights beckon, but we'd have to be cockroaches to negotiate that joke of a broken bridge. I'll starve on this blasted rock, staring at my grave while some backpedaling egghead lectures me on subterranean geomorphology. There's an irony lurking in here somewhere. Maybe it's just too dim to see it."

Amantu stamped a sandaled foot, so great was his vexation. "There is but one source of dimness! Nearly forty years have I fumed behind the lectern, only to stand here—babysitting another spoiled child. Just when clear thinking is requisite, again rises that gut-wrenching wail of the comfort-bereaved. How you have juggled a career, *Doctor* Weaver, is a mystery to me. Do your patients arrive for sessions with kerchiefs in hand?"

"That'll be about enough of that. At least my people are above arrogance."

"I? Arrogant? Well, '*Izzy*,' it requires a full measure of humility to tolerate your multitudinous plaints and petty outbursts. That I so recently called you friend is now an outrage even to myself. Your narrow-minded, self-pitying utterances are untenable."

"Did I say arrogance? Well, I meant *ignorance!* Ignorance of geography! Ignorance of teamwork! Ignorance of even the rudiments of humanity."

"And *that*, sir, will be about enough of that! I deem it only fair to warn you: my patience has been tried unduly. I am a thinking man, not a reactive one. But—so help me!"

Izzy nearly lost his balance pushing himself to his feet. His forward position on the smooth rock's incline increased his disadvantage in relation to the bigger man, so that now his raised eyes were barely at the level of Amantu's sternum. "Your patience!" He scooted upward with difficulty, sliding back an inch for every three gained, until he and Amantu were facing one another perpendicularly to the apertures; the weak light setting one side of their frames aglow, the other side remaining in bleary shadow. Still the smaller man by half a head, Izzy began to cheat, inching up and around until he and the professor were eye to eye. With his very black face eclipsing an aperture, Amantu became a pair of white floating eyes against the lesser darkness. "*Your* patience!" Izzy repeated. "Have you *any idea* how frustrating this is for me? To meekly abide, in front of my learned friends...to play along with an awkward braggadocio—*solely* to spare him further embarrassment!"

"Enough," Amantu snarled.

Increasing his advantage by raising himself on his toes, Izzy mocked the professor's basso profundo with biting accuracy. "'I heartily approve of this plan, AJ!' *Well*, Professor Emeritus, I think I can hear Josh cursing us rather heartily even now!"

"Enough!"

But Izzy was on a roll. "'Oh, just follow *me*, Doctor Weaver! *Exploration*, Doctor Weaver, is a grand feature of my oh-so noble lineage. Doctor Weaver, it is in my *genes*'!"

"*Enough!*" And with that, triggered by a lifetime of being odd man out, the Hammer came down. The heavyset professor could have inflicted considerable damage with this one roundhouse punch, but he was swinging uphill, and his balance was off. The next thing he knew he was spread-eagled flat on his belly, rigid fingers desperately seeking purchase on the smooth rock's face while he very gradually slipped into eternity.

Izzy dropped immediately and grabbed the professor's wrists. Amantu instinctively copied the hold. "Mercy!" Izzy cried, as the heavier man's weight pulled him along.

Amantu bellowed, "Do *not* struggle!" Both men froze, cutouts plastered on stone.

"Find a foothold!" Izzy cried, his nose banging on the rock with each hard consonant. "For Christ's sake, Hammer!" He and the professor slid an inch.

Amantu forced back his head, "There *is* none!" And down they slid, a foot and more. The men stopped struggling, stopped speaking, stopped breathing.

Now Amantu was holding on using only the pressure of his thighs. All feeling rolled down his arms to his quaking heart. The certainty of death took him, and for a moment he was a breath away from fainting.

"Professor," Izzy gagged. "I...I...*can't.*"

Abruptly the cavern's light was cut to a fraction. In the apertures were two peaked silhouettes, with accompanying coronas. A torch was thrust through each opening. Out rang the unmistakable voice of Micah. "Zounds, Easy! What lovers *will* do when the lights are low!"

"Sirs!" Amantu snapped. And with that he and Izzy scraped down another half-foot. *"Anything!"*

Micah and Ezekiel hopped across the bridge easily; a torch in one hand, an arm momentarily embracing each rain-rounded peak. They perched upon the final cap to taunt the anxious men, a yard from the rock and two feet below Amantu's quivering sandals.

"Show him that face you make, Easy. The one with the torch."

With the sputtering brand beneath his raised chin, Ezekiel was the Grim Reaper personified. He grimaced and gnashed, his red-tinged hood flapping. "Whoo-*oo*-ooo! I'm gonna get you, you nasty atheists, you. Whoo-*oo*-oo!"

Micah roared with laughter, then shook the professor's

foot while doing a spirited jig on the lip of infinity.

"I beg you," Amantu whispered. "I can hold no longer."

"Lucky for you we happened by. Me and Easy was just strolling along, making with the mandibles, when we heared what sounded like a pair of ginger cats in heat. Had us a peek through the tribe's windows and—oh, Lord, I about blushed with the sight of ye. I just thank the Good Almighty we arrived in the nick of time." He lifted the professor's tattered robe and walked his fingers up the calf.

Amantu kicked involuntarily. His nails dug deeper into Izzy's wrists and the two slid another foot. "Cease, pervert! We are in dire need!"

"Pervy, am I? Just who's wearing the pretty gold party dress, that's what I'd be asking m'self about now." He lifted the robe again and, standing on tiptoes, ran his fingers right up the back of Amantu's thigh.

This playful act, to a man of such propriety, was an unspeakable violation. Utilizing forgotten muscles in his fore-arms and thighs, the bellowing professor shot up the rock like a spider, hauling Izzy with him. Micah and Ezekiel roared with laughter and set their torches in niches chipped out for just such a climb. "We'll make rockers of ye yet, missies!"

Flat on their backs, the doctor and professor peered be-tween their knees as Micah and Ezekiel picked their way up, utilizing handholds only now visible.

"Pagans, pagans," the frighteners sang, "all fall down!"

Backing up frantically, Amantu and Izzy were aston-ished to see Abel's face pop out below the grinning climbers. Both monsters whirled at the displacement of torchlight.

"*Ha!*" Izzy yelped. "Turnabout!"

"That's right," chattered Abel, thrusting the torches left and right. "I warned you guys last time. Don't force me. I'll burn you if I have to."

"A wholly qualified sentiment!" Amantu crowed. "These men are psychopaths!"

The climbers exchanged glances. Micah bluffed a kick. Ezekiel followed up with the real thing. Abel parried with the right-hand torch and went straight for Ezekiel's lancing right leg with the other. The ragged old robe caught instantly. Ezekiel beat at the racing flames, lost his balance, and flew screaming off the rock back-first. Down he went like a comet, blazing all the way.

Micah stared bitterly before switching his gaze to a high stalagmite just beyond that critical peak now occupied by Abel. He kicked off his perch, sailed over Abel's torches like a huge black witch, and landed on all fours with the nimbleness of a bighorn. He righted himself soundlessly, glared at the awestruck Group, and went hopping and swaying back along the bridge of stalagmites. At the apertures he drew himself erect, cutting out half the light and breathing hard. His eyes burned in his silhouetted hood. Then he was gone.

With the rock's face lit by torches, its chipped-out handholds became plainly visible. Even so, it was the hardest thing in the world to coach the stranded men down. Izzy, as the lightest, had to come first—Abel could catch him when he jumped, while both he and Izzy were required for the larger professor. But for Izzy, who saw Ezekiel's death as an augur, the simple three-foot hop onto the nearest cap was an ordeal that made Abel scream himself silly. Even when he had hold of the doctor's arms it was a fight to peel him off the big rock, and in the end only Amantu's weight on his shoulders could make Izzy release his wide embrace. The professor himself made the little leap with a surprising nimbleness.

Abel had memorized Micah's holds and turns across the tricky stalagmite bridge. The men moved delicately, feeling their way up and around each peak before swinging over to the next, then spontaneously turned for panting congratulations on a ledge below the twin openings. Izzy puffed up and offered his paw all around. "They were wrong to underestimate the Group."

Amantu shook it well. "And a most formidable Group we are." He was uniquely moved when Abel's hand completed the knot. "Well!" He pulled his hand away and, to conceal his embarrassment, poked his head out into the light.

Chapter Ten

Evolution

T he professor found himself studying a vast cave lit by torches spaced every ten feet. Walls were painted with smudged charcoal, depicting unfamiliar scenes of black stick figures engaged in erroneous battle. In the floor's dead-center was a low lake, apparently composed of tar or pitch, encircled by at least a hundred skin lean-tos. Mock-nativity scenes filled these half-shacks; scarecrow families, mangers of sticks and trash. Crosses were soot-painted up and down the leaning buildings' outer walls.

Isolated on a rocky knoll stood a small, roofless, kiln-like structure surrounded by stack upon stack of charred branches. The cave's roof above this little building must have been two feet deep with soot. There wasn't a soul about. Abel's and Izzy's heads poked out the other aperture. The men all exchanged glances before ducking back inside.

"Deserted," Amantu whispered.

Abel shook his head. "It's where that costumed creep went, and you just know he's pissed. It's a trap; that's why it's so quiet."

"Fortunately, this is one instance wherein lengthy discussion is obviated. We cannot retrace our steps, we must see this turn as a boon and proceed undaunted."

After a moment Abel nodded. "Hear, hear." He turned to Izzy.

"Too quiet!" The analyst shrank before them, licking his lips. "You're right, Josh. No, no, I agree with Hammer! No, no, no…*wait!* Let's work this out."

Abel grabbed him by the belt and collar. "One side, Professor. I'm stuffing this little pimiento." He shoved Izzy through headfirst, aided, perhaps a bit vindictively, by Amantu. The Group huddled behind a short screen of boulders.

"Not limestone," Amantu panted. "Both caverns were formed through the action of seepage, but this side lacked the calcium carbonate. That lake appears to be either vented crude or a tar pit."

"Not so." Abel indicated a black channel beaten out of the rock, running from the little building down to the lake. "It's rain water stained by liquefied charcoal."

"Balls descending," Izzy whispered. "To what end?"

As if cued, a pair of huge coiled spiders dropped from an overhead ledge, landing in the heart of the little crescent formed by the men. They sprang up screaming, revealing themselves to be naked children all but coated in lampblack—only the white masks of their faces, and the crude skeletal outlines on their torsos and limbs, were unpainted. These boys immediately began dancing about like the rudest of monkeys; pointing, shrieking, making obscene noises with their mouths. The men kept low against the wall as they retreated, but the youngsters were relentless in their hooting pursuit. Soon the Group were locked in among heaped rocks and the wall: three grown men cowed by a couple of obnoxious brats. In the distance commenced a great cry, followed by the quick thunder of running feet.

A crowd of adults appeared, calling to the hopping children in modulated hoots as they ran. These folks were likewise painted with soot, and all showed old welt scars across their backs and limbs. Self-mutilation was a tribal theme; there were women with rat ribs plunged into cheeks and throats, men bearing their own amputated toes strung round their necks like good luck charms. One particularly unappealing gentleman boasted a pair of sharp stones crammed up his nostrils, a wife with a porcupine-like collection of bone spurs pounded through her tongue into the lower palate, and a pair of children minus lips and eyelids. All the women, according to the wont of their gender, used soot ornamentally, creating rings, crescents, and whorls around their most private areas. To the men of civilization, the result was anything but comely.

Over two dozen teenagers shoved through the gawkers. Their leader's face was startling, unforgettable, and just as pathetic as it was frightening. The eyes were permanently raccoon-ringed from bashings, the mouth a lopsided, gummy snarl, the nose—smashed flat from the center out—a broad, mangled flap. After so much punishment, this young man had to be unimaginably tough to keep his lieutenants close and his contenders at their distance. That fiber was evinced now, as he strode right up to Amantu and stared him up and down. The professor slowly rose to his full height and their eyes locked. Ever so gradually, the young man raised his fist until it was hovering halfway between them, made a right angle of his wrist, and swiveled the fist like a cobra's head. Never had Amantu imagined knuckles so scarred. The professor instinctively closed his eyes an instant before the young man pulled back the fist and punched himself in the nose as hard as he could.

Amantu's eyes popped open. Though that smashed-in face was gushing blood, the expression hadn't changed a line. To their right, a trio of youngsters responded with an all-out slugfest.

"Off it!" the bleeding young man spewed. The little ruffians immediately broke up. He turned back, holding Amantu's eyes like the fiercer of strays. "Could *you* do that?" He socked himself in the face again. The nose-flap surrendered a spurt and trickle. He hit himself repeatedly, with mounting ferocity. "How about that? And that? And *that*?" The crowd went nuts. Men slapped and gouged themselves with mindless machismo, women shook their stuff hysterically. A young man ripped out a clump of hair, another viciously twisted an ear that had become, through years of abuse, a shapeless string of hanging taffy.

"Smite him!" called a voice in the rear.

The chant began. "Smite him, smite him, smite him."

"*Off* it!" the leader sobbed. He punched himself furiously, until the professor bellowed,

"*Cease!*" Everybody froze. Amantu squared himself. "What is your name, lad?"

The young man spat blood between them. "It's Samp-sun. After the baddest cat in the Book." He rocked back and forth aggressively. "My boys call me Sammy. But to the likes of *you,* it's Sampsun."

"Well, *Sammy,* I too have a nickname, earned from more humbled students than I care to enumerate. They call me 'Old Iron Hand.' But behind my back, mind you, always behind my back. Now, rather than demonstrate this sobriquet's origin, I shall acquiesce to you, sir, and without further confrontation. I hereby deem you the 'badder cat' of we two. And, if it will abet mollification, I will go so far as to admit you are the toughest man I have ever known."

The human monkeys screamed, and a moment later were both dancing maniacally. The crowd turned. Without breaking his stare, Sampsun sprayed a mouthful of blood on Amantu's chin and breast.

"Then slap on a clean toga, Senator. Because here comes the man."

"Sir—"

"Slew you, buddy!"

The professor squirmed. "The correct tense would indi-cate the transitive verb, 'slay'."

"Yeah? Well, slew you anyway!"

The crowd parted.

It was easy to see what made the tribe's leader their top dog. He approached with regal slowness, his haughty head held high, vacillating, like a man on stilts, on intricately whittled stalactite crutches. Children swept him a serpentine path while an entourage of women gingerly walked his terribly bowed legs. The Group members gasped with horror and disbelief as he neared, instinctively crossing their knees.

The chief had earned his office by fitting, at some time during his superhuman ascent, a calcite sculpture designed to relentlessly strangle his gonads, now swollen to the size of grapefruits. The tenderness of these organs made unassisted locomotion impossible, made his trembly legs buckle and bounce, made his bleary eyes flicker. But nothing could quash this man's spirit. Upon reaching the Group, he pushed himself upright, and his eyes ran over the quailing trespassers with the contempt of a born superior.

"So they sent us women, did they? And a foppish phalanx at that." The chief pivoted man to man, flashes raging in his pupils at each contact of crutch on ground. He clicked to a halt before Amantu, fascinated by the stranger's ebony flesh and vivid attire. Sampsun, following his boss's every move, spooned right up behind the professor and locked arms. The chief pressed his white mask forward until he and Amantu were nose to nose. "What land," he whispered loudly, "produceth a man so dark? Or is it just your black nature? Could it be you're the demon his Self? Well, then? What do they call you?"

Amantu looked the chief right in his swimming eyes. "*I*, sir, am known as the Hammer."

The chief looked around, laughing lustily. He hoisted one of his sculpted crutches and shook it in Amantu's face. "Now *that*, sir, is a hammer!"

Much cheering and rib-nudging.

The professor must have flinched, for the crowd pressed in keenly.

"Who sent you?" the chief demanded.

"Sir, we were abducted into this place. We have no quarrel with you or your people. Grant us our freedom and we will exit with grace. You will have our undying gratitude."

"Grace!" The man shook with umbrage. *"Grace!"* He grabbed a crutch by the shaft and, incredibly, slammed it straight up between his legs. The chief let go with a scream that tore through every male within earshot. He hit the ground like a bomb. In a conditioned response, all the men and boys dropped and rolled about shrieking, their hands tucked between their knees.

The Group doubled over. The tribesmen leaped back up cheering.

"Enough," Izzy moaned, stamping a foot. "Oh, Mercies! Enough already!"

The chief's women lifted him into the cradle of their arms. He hung there like a squid in a net, sweat pouring off his face. Finally his eyes rolled back up. He grasped a crutch and aimed it for his nethers.

"No!" the Group yelled, withering in advance.

"Anything!" cried Abel. "*Anything!* Yes, we're 'demons!' Yes, we're spies! Only—no more!"

The crutch rose an inch.

"Sir," Amantu began, "I implore you—" He was cut off by another scream from the chief: the second upward thrust was already underway. This time, however, the man was too spent to complete the deed, and found himself propped with his arms dangling, the crutch supporting his listing torso. Now the Group were the hysterical howlers, and the tribesmen the anxious observers. The chief's women threw themselves into a swooning dance while Sammy, beside himself, frantically punched himself in the face and, for good measure, attacked the recoiling face of each Group member in turn. The chief appeared to take heart in the mindless violence, raising himself an inch with each smack of fist into flesh. At last he squealed, "*Messiah,*" grabbed the shaft with both hands, and delivered himself the wallop of his career. The whole crowd dropped as one, every male rolling about in the fetal position while wailing wretchedly. In a choreographed response, the women reversed their collapse, drawing themselves erect in a complicated counterclockwise ballet that culminated in a group cruciform stance, hands holding hands, eyes raised beatifically.

"Off it *all!*"

The women froze, the males wobbled to their feet. Sammy bent to whisper in the chief's ear, tilted his head for the reply, and shot back up, his expression triumphant. "The Bathsmith!"

"*John!*" the people all chanted deliriously. "John! John! *John*-John!" Sammy thereupon launched himself on the released Group, his fists flying. But one man on three is a minor assault; Amantu and Abel, using Izzy for a shield, easily knocked him back.

Now the spiders ran up to the rocky knoll, screaming all the way. They blew in through the little structure's hide flap and blew back out, joyously dancing round a tar-colored child balancing a long sputtering torch, and a very tall, very thin, very bald man in his forties. Unlike the rest of the tribe, John was daubed black head to toe. Only his raving eyes showed white. In his gangly fingers rocked a massive tome constructed entirely of human parchment, so heavy with lampblack it puffed as he strode. This would be the fabulous Black Book, its skin pages meticulously sewn, char-painted, and scribed in urine only made visible through the heat of the Sacred Torch.

John stormed out onto a little projecting bank of the lake. There he stood with the Book raised high in both hands, impaling the Group with his furious eyes. After an agonizing two minutes he plunged the Book to knee-level with finality.

"*On* it!" Sammy exuberated, and ran off to join John while the tribe's males bullied the Group toward a small shallow cove.

"Mind your hands!" Abel barked, beginning to crack.

"You shut your face!" hissed a nineteen year-old, slapping him twice on the ear. The younger boys reacted excitedly, one chewing on Izzy's leg as the doctor was dragged along wailing.

Amantu's left wrist was jammed up between his shoulder blades. *"Desist!"*

"Rot in Hades," a youngster replied.

"Where?" Abel gasped, fighting the dark fingers.

"You know where!" claimed another, striking him directly on the tailbone. The Group were hauled kicking and cursing into the murky pool.

At the first touch of wetness the professor threw off his handlers. "*Listen*, you people! You are deluded. There is no plague; you are not carriers. We have *all* been bamboozled." A hand slapped him across the face. Amantu froze. It took every ounce of self-control to feign calm, and to say reasonably, "You are not responsible for your lives or behaviour. Leave this world. Follow us back into the light."

Abel took a faceful of black water. "It's no use, Hammer. You're only provoking them. Reason, in a madhouse, is insanity."

The youngsters took delight in tormenting Izzy; pinching and slapping his legs and buttocks whenever they could get their hands on him. When he fell in the ooze they immediately hauled him to his feet. "Josh is right!" the little psychoanalyst gagged. "So everybody just shut up and let this thing play itself out."

Abel and Amantu paused, shoulder-to-shoulder, waist-deep and surrounded. It was an odd experience to look into two dozen flesh masks, each revealing, in the intricate application of lampblack, a distinct and perfectly flawed human personality. One teenager shied before giving Abel a particularly nasty look. "What are *you* staring at, pretty boy? See something you like?" His buddies laughed nervously.

Amantu and Abel exchanged glances. Picking up on the vibe, Izzy joined them in a closer study of the savage circle.

Many of the younger adults had decorated overzealously around the lips and eyes, and practically all the teens bore similarly-shaped blotches on their upper right foreheads. Vanity, gang affiliation, marginal effeminacy...disdain remade the Group's expressions. The ring clenched and fidgeted. Under the hard light of intellectual censure for the very first time, some of those tough eyes began to slink away. The Group put their backs together and rose out of the water like men.

A hard command from Sammy preceded a sudden splashing and a couple of slaps. Two teens broke the ring to admit the Bathsmith and his best boy.

John towered over the circle. Only his rolling eyeballs and gnashing teeth were not covered with soot; even the lids and lips were blackened. His boy, up to his neck in murk, awkwardly balanced the heavy Book on his nose, using his palms to support the opened halves. For a moment it looked as though the weight of the thing would submerge him, but he bravely straightened and goggled at his master over the Black Book's rim.

At a signal from Sammy, the anxiously waiting monkeys came tumbling and screaming down the grade, one behind the other, passing the flaming Torch back and forth as they changed positions. Upon reaching the water, the ritual became a scrabbling struggle for possession, quickly broken up by a couple of hard smacks from John. Sammy seized the torch and moved it to and fro while the Bathsmith tore at the Book's heavy skin leaves, looking for commandments that dealt specifically with intellectuals. Finding none, he slammed the Black Book shut and raised his left hand high before dashing it across the filthy water. "Chris!" he cried. Abel and Izzy hacked as they were fouled by spray. A second later John's right hand splashed Amantu. "Cross!"

Now a terrible silence enveloped the circle. With great drama, John gradually raised his arms in tandem, his eyes popping in his skull. The instant his fingertips touched, he brought both hands down hard on the water. *"Double-Cross!"*

Roaring with approval, the human ring leapt on their prisoners' backs, shoved them down and held them down. Any man managing to break surface was immediately swarmed and pressed back under. This wasn't some kind of ritualistic punishment; it was serious business. The Group were being drowned. The more they thrashed and kicked, the more determinedly their executioners piled on. When again they were brought into the air, they were barely aware of the fists in their hair, and of the voices of Micah and Malachi above them.

The professor lurched along the bank, vomiting black ooze from his mouth and nostrils. Micah held down his head until the spasms were passed, then shook him by a handful of robe. He yanked up both the Hammer's and Izzy's heads, smashed their skulls together, and pushed his lips down right between their ears. "You're a bushel more trouble than you're worth, Senators! And *I*, for *one*, am filthy *sick*, and stinking *tired*, of chasey-chasing you all over the place! You *got* me? Now, I *told* you you're going to see the Possle, and, damn you all to Hades and back, you're *going* to see the Possle!"

Chapter Eleven

The Possle

The Group put up no resistance as they were dragged down one long tunnel after another. Even in his semiconscious state, Amantu was aware of an overall increase in brightness as they progressed, and more torches could only mean they were nearing the nest. Micah and Malachi savagely kicked off the groping inhabitants, but not out of fear for their own safety—these lunging men and women were vying solely for a fist or a foot in the face. It was clear, by the tenor of the bullies' cursing, that this was all a frustrating routine of Honeycomb navigation. Eventually the flow grew to a scrabbling riot, obliging Micah to clear a path with a torch to the eyes of anyone near. When the smell of singed flesh became unbearable he handed his brand to Malachi, yanked Amantu to his feet, and slapped the professor's cheeks back and forth until he began to weakly struggle. Micah shoved him face-first at random grappling souls.

"See anybody like him in the big city? *Huh*, Mr. Filthy Godless Atheist? Or how's about her? You got anyone that tough in your sissy-arse offices? And how long d'you think you, without a sheep or a shepherd, could last down here? Let *me* learn *you* something, brainy-boy. God don't like gray matter, he ain't above a little *apropos* torture now and then, and He sure ain't partial to guys in gold skirts." Micah twisted Amantu's arm up behind his back until the professor bellowed with pain. "I'll learn you something else. The Book says a long-long time ago they had someones called gladiators. You know why they was so glad? Because they got to go out and slew one another for sport and big hurrahs. Let me tell you, *Senator*, they was some tough pickles back then; men who really knew how to get God's attention. Now, it occurs to both me and Mal that He might be wanting to see what stuff you're made of, once we get you into a fighting mood proper."

"Twenty-t—" called Malachi, "—twenty t-talons on the f-fat one."

"Which?" said Micah.

"Biggest!"

"Not a chance. She's my pretty bull." He caressed Amantu's recoiling cheek with the back of his hand. "Thirty."

"On wh-who?"

"Little one."

"Twenty f-five and dirty-d—dirty-d—dirty d-doubles!"

"On!" Micah blew into Amantu's sweat-soaked hair. "You won't disappoint me now, will you, sugar? I knows good fighting blood when I smells it."

Malachi prodded Izzy over, grabbed a couple of torches, and cleared a space by singeing anyone within reach. In a minute the place was reeling with screams and the stench of burnt hair. After adamantly whispering in Izzy's ear, Micah walked back to Amantu, jabbing a finger repeatedly at Abel as he strode. "Watch *him!*" Malachi obediently busied himself with Abel. Micah yanked back the professor's head.

"Okay," he breathed. "We's all set. You two meets in the center and you kicks the fat boy in the nuts just once. *Don't let him do you back!* I told him you'd be instructed to faint-and-perry, so he won't be ready. It's what we calls 'a internal double-cross,' just like what you done on him what taked it for us." His eyes sizzled. "*You* remember how to pull a fast one now, *don't* you, Senator?"

The prisoners were pushed face to face. Malachi released Izzy, who stood sagging like an abandoned marionette. "Right in the nuts!" Micah hissed, and backed away.

After half a minute Izzy opened his puffy, oil-soaked eyes. Trembling all over, he threw out his arms, sobbed, "Oh...*Hammer!*" and fell into the professor's wide embrace.

"F-f-forfeit!" Malachi screamed, stamping in circles

while Amantu stroked Izzy's filthy crown.

"Forfeit my hoary white arse!" Micah socked Amantu upside the head. The professor didn't budge. Cussing up a storm, the brute tore off his gloves and reached past a torn-gold shoulder for Izzy's collar. He was absolutely stunned when Amantu, still gripping Izzy in one arm, turned half-around and backhanded him right across the face. The two stood chin to chin, their eyes locked.

"Know good fighting blood," the Hammer said evenly, "when you smell it."

Malachi shrieked with anticipation. Picking up on the excitement, the hundreds of babbling crawlers made for the source, mucking up the ring in the process. Malachi waded through the prostrate swarm hissing, braining as many as he could reach with a torch-head.

"Sometime," Micah mumbled. "Sometime soon." He grabbed an old man and worked him over furiously for Malachi's sake, watching the stalwart professor all the while. Amantu turned away. With Malachi distracted, Abel was able to join his friends. The reformed Group, cowed by torches, were knocked wall-to-wall through the mob like caroming billiard balls. The flow halted at the opening to a low, unlit cave, where men and women began flogging themselves and coughing out strange garbled sentences, apparently directed to the tiny cave's interior. Inside it was absolutely black. Micah threw his left arm around Amantu's neck, his right arm around the necks of Abel and Izzy, and pulled all three together until the men's crowns were touching. He was an immensely strong man, and he stank terribly, even in this foul place. He laid his bone-white chin on the moist nest of their contiguous heads and called into the little hole.

"We gone and captured us the Barberus! Caught him and his pretty fairy-mates up in the Citydel. He's been taked to the Stone Hollow now, but Mama'll be wanting the little-dots on these three flitty-flight fancies." He gave Amantu a big smacking kiss on his hot wooly crown, and with that the Group were kicked headlong into the dark. They immediately drew into a tight seated huddle, panting frantically, nursing their sores while their eyes adjusted. Bad as it was outside, this little hell-hole reeked vilely. Micah, crouching in the entrance, spat out, "Don't even *think* about leaving till he's done with you! You make us chase you again and I swears to the almighty Soul we'll put an end to you, splickety-splat, and right where we catches ye. So keeps your butts level, and your eyes straight ahead. We'll be right here waiting, and boy, will we be watching." At a barked command, Malachi hunched just outside the cave's mouth, using his spread cloak to block the light.

Izzy shuddered as he clung. "This abuse must end! I can't brea—I can't brea—I can't brea—"

"Hang on, man!" Abel whispered. "I'm right here."

Izzy slapped him furiously. "*'Right here!'* Where were you ten minutes ago, when I and the Hammer were standing off a madman?"

Abel smacked him right back. "Getting my teeth singed, you miserable little turncoat." He craned and squinted in the dark. "What did he mean, 'done with' us? Until *who's* done with us?"

The Group froze. A primitive dread of dens and lairs made them read strange shapes out of common contours. Every little nook and protuberance demanded varying measures of attention, but soon all eyes were fixed on a single, too-regular bulge that seemed to be pumping out of the pitch.

The Possle approached in lunges and slithers, his grotesque body dipping and rising side-to-side. He was unable to move otherwise, as all four limbs had been amputated long ago, leaving simple chubby outgrowths at the shoulders and hips. There were no eyes, only black sockets that appeared to search the dark. As the men backed away the heaving horror froze, and for perhaps half a minute the head felt the cave, rolling left and right a centimeter at a time. It took Abel to break the silence.

"You poor wretch. Who did this to you?"

The Possle came directly at him, waving his stumps for balance. When he was a yard away he stopped and raised his head like a sea lion. His struggles to articulate were expressed in sucks and whistles.

"Mama say Possle stay, serve Mama: good limb make bad Possle. Mama say Possle not see elsewhere: good eye see bad thing. Mama say Possle talk too much." He showed them the wagging nub of his severed tongue. "Now good Possle." He flopped round to each man in turn. "Mama say Possle test all man—one man, two man, three. All man three man—sell thief to Punchus Pilot. Mama say thief belong Mama."

"Oh Mercies!" Izzy cried. "Shake me! Wake me!"

The Possle wheeled on his belly, his ears pricked.

"Ti...tus...Mack," Abel over-enunciated. *"Friend.* Friend of three man." The Possle's head swiveled at the thorax. "The man's no thief, for Christ's sake. He's a brilliant astronomer. All this nonsense is ingrained behavior. You people are chasing shadows."

The Possle bumped noses. "Mama say thief belong Mama!"

Abel recoiled from the stench. "Well, tell her he's ours, damn you! And let us go. He needs medical attention."

Izzy rocked back and forth, his forearms clamped against his ears. "Oh, man! Oh, *man!* Oh man, oh man, oh man! Who, or what, is *Mama?"*

The Possle bobbed as he nodded. "Mama Mary. Mary Mama. Messiah marry Mama. Rat eat Messiah. Mama gnaw, Mama gnaw." With a horrible snuffling sound, the Possle did a nose-dive, slamming his face straight into the ground. When he looked back up, scuffed and bleeding, his feral expression was twisted into something like joy. "Good God! God good! God make Mary! God make Messiah! God make Possle!"

Abel's eyes burned in the dark. "What *God?* It's like we've been trying to tell you people—you've been suckered. We've *all* been suckered! There is no supernature; it's an old fairy tale. Your behavior *belowground* is the consequence of a primitive set of tenets contrived *aboveground.*" He straightened and scooched forward. "Now *you're* gonna listen to *me,* pal!

"A long time ago a mob of religious morons followed some politically-embarrassed lunatic, and he convinced them to smash up our entire technological system. He brought a bunch of them down here, where they adhered to his senile rewrite of their codification, which was probably a pretty good thing before the idiot bastardized it. All *this* crap grew out of all *that* crap! For Christ's sake, man—get to a schoolhouse, get to a hospital, get to a loony bin. Izzy, give him your card."

The Possle's head ratcheted around and he began to rock in a slow, contemplative spiral.

"Um, Josh," Izzy mumbled. "This is probably the last guy we need to antagonize right now. I recognize the symptoms." He smiled and raised his voice. "We're just having a friendly little confab here, not a dialogue. Isn't that so, Mr. Possle?" He grinned until it hurt, spreading his arms high and wide. "We all know there's a God. He's just kind of hard to see in all this darkness, that's all."

"God *here*," the Possle insisted, rolling side to side to indicate universality. Coupled with his meditative rocking, the rolling threw him into a short tailspin. His brain locked up. After a long, creepy minute he snapped out of it and rose bolt-upright. "God good! Good God! God create Colony. God give Possle all this."

Abel blew it. "Good! *Good?* How...*dare* you! What kind of fu—what sort—*what manner of divinity would sanction such suffering?*"

The Possle stopped rocking.

Amantu broke in hurriedly. "One divinely apologetic, of that I am certain! A holy line, you say! A dynasty? That is most—that is inde*scrib*ably fascinating! Please press on, Mr. Possle. Do tell us more."

The Possle jounced about until he was facing the professor, moved his head up and down and all around. It took Amantu a minute to realize he was being sniffed. The head moved in closer. When that nauseating countenance was only six inches away, the eye sockets seemed to deepen and the mouth opened wide. The Possle fell into a cobra-like swaying, mesmerized by his own stupidity. Using only his pelvic muscles, he drew himself upright and bobbed at each man in turn.

"Judas one, Judas two, Judas three! All Judas go Mama!"

"But," Amantu tried. "*Sir.* It is not our intention to interf—"

"*Judas!*" the Possle screamed. "Mama, Mama! Judas, Judas! Mama, Mama!" Malachi stepped aside, allowing light to flood the cave. "Judas, Judas!" the Possle wailed. "Mama,

Mama!" Now a nervous clamor arose in the tunnel, growing in volume and passion with each repetition:

"Mama, *Mama!* Mama, *Mama!*"

"That'll do 'er!" said Micah. He and Malachi scrambled in, thrusting their torches at the turning men. The big man waved his directly in the Possle's face. The Group shied. "Told you he was a looker. Now, up on your twos, you nasty nihilists. We's off to the Cavalry, and when we—"

He was cut off by an explosive surge at the cave entrance. Men and women were fighting to squeeze inside, their arms and faces flapping about like the tentacles of sea anemones. "Judas all!" the Possle shrieked. The plug of bodies went mad.

Micah stuck his torch in the Possle's nightmarish face. "Shut your hole!" Malachi used his own torch to press back the crowd, and, once the entrance was cleared, Micah kicked the Group out one by one. He grabbed Amantu's collar and shoved him against the tunnel wall. "It's party time, you big sweet parasite. Cross your knees and prays you dies, 'cause *you* gots a date with Mama."

"Mama!"

And Abel and Izzy were riding a wave of rabid humanity, with Malachi scrabbling underfoot. Off to the side, Micah was driving Amantu by ramming him against the wall with his right shoulder, then ricocheting to clear their path with his left. The professor regained his focus as they ran. On one of these inward thrusts he surprised Micah by grabbing his arm and using the impetus to send him slamming into the hot rock. Micah recovered quickly, snatching Amantu's arm in kind and flinging him at the naked flow. Amantu was knocked right back at him. The two found themselves whirling in and out of the mass, banging hard against the walls, spinning into the fray. Conditioned reflex caused those nearest to be thrown into fits of passion; they struck themselves and one another, bit at arms and legs. There was a minute of complete confusion; of slipping on rolling limbs and flailing every which way, and then Micah and Amantu were toe-to-toe and nose-to-nose, both heavyweights throwing bombs to the head that neither man felt. A wild left from Amantu tore off Micah's hood, ripping out the staples and revealing the balding, very human psychopath beneath. He followed up with a roundhouse right to the ear that sent the brute sprawling among a flurry of stampeding legs. Micah bounded back to his feet with his bleeding face ablaze, his hands scrabbling for the professor's eyes. And now, for the first time in his life, Amantu just snapped. He whaled blindly with both fists until a random haymaker caught the giant on the jaw and put him flat on his back. The professor came down hard, straddling Micah's chest. The two went rolling underfoot, and when they surfaced in the muddle each had the other by the throat.

For the longest time both squeezed furiously without breathing. Micah was sprawled on his back, his head propped on a rock, Amantu's knees planted squarely beside his ribs. The fighters' faces darkened, their snarls widened, their screaming eyes bugged out in a death struggle that went way beyond personal survival. When Amantu felt himself going, he blew out his razor breath, jerked up his arms to break Micah's grip, and slammed both locked fists straight down on the monster's rising purple face.

The force of the blow split Micah's skull on the stone like a ripe pomegranate, turning his raging expression into a meek splash of passive surprise. Blood spewed from his mouth and nostrils, his chin shot out at an angle, his eyes rolled back in his skull. Amantu heaved himself off and staggered into the mob.

Abel and Izzy went bobbing by on a raft of shoulders. Amantu croaked out their names, but in the din was unsure he heard himself. There had to be a thousand people fighting along like spawning salmon, all crying out, *"Mama!"* in the manner of retarded children. Amantu laid into the crashing bodies; first out of desperation, then out of rage and disgust. The hot sweaty flesh smacked his mouth and eyes, the raving faces made him snarl as he swung.

He came stumbling into the brightly lit Heart without realizing it, still throwing his fists indiscriminately. The human flow ceased abruptly at the entrance, so that Amantu appeared to be ejected, rather than self-propelled, from its midst. Hordes of immature rats swarmed past him, followed by a peppery explosion of hissing and squealing bats, but the professor hardly noticed. He was utterly exhausted. Any man in his condition would have instinctively grabbed at whatever would stand him, but the scene in that chamber was so mind-boggling—nothing could be so...never had he imagined...Amantu's whole frame collapsed and he dropped to his knees.

Chapter Twelve

Mama

he Heart was a huge amphitheater-like depression, complete with a flat raised stage covered with the sacred skeletal remains of tortured and hanged Honeycomb Rats. There were wall niches for a hundred sputtering torches. The stage's convex bluff featured letters carved four feet high, spelling out the word CAVALRY.

Three cruciform figures dominated this stage, each with an identifying name chiseled in small caps. *Chris* was a four-foot cross of rusted pipe lengths, situated nearest the cavern entrance. *Cross*, a posted leaning six-footer at center stage, had been fashioned of thousands of bone fragments sewn with lengths of human hair. *Double-Cross* was a large cross-shaped hollow, with matching shackles and complementary blood gutter, chipped out of the far wall.

Hunched at the foot of *Double-Cross*, Abel and Izzy were frantically administering to a mortally injured Titus Mack, now wearing only a bramble crown and a filthy rag wound up like a diaper. *Double-Cross*, by the wrist shackles and blood stains in the hollow, was obviously a stoning platform. And Mack, by his bashed appearance and wretched collapse, had just as obviously received the full treatment.

Chris, a spooky affair, supported a complete human skeleton, char-painted overall except for the broken teeth and polished cave pearl eyes. The blacked bones of this skeleton, like the cross itself, were attached by long strands of woven human hair. There was hair everywhere; strung into decorative coils and streamers, hung about like cobwebs from walls that glistened with layers of plastered human fat. The stench of that burnt hair permeated the Honeycomb Heart.

Tied to the skeleton's clavicle, one end of a long hair-rope passed through its skull and out a hole bored in the cap, causing the dreadful bone monster to dance about grinning when the opposite end was pulled. This rope threaded a steel ring in the rock ceiling, and thence passed down to the central *Cross*, where it terminated in a noose around the scrawny neck framed by Madame Rat's great waving mane of ash-white hair.

Mama was an emaciated nude woman in her nineties, nailed to a cross of sewn tibias and femurs. Every square inch of the woman's epidermis had been attacked by lash and stone, so that now her body was a red and purple monstrosity; half-healed at the sites of recent abominations, waxy pink from the lingering kisses of countless torches. Mama's eyes had been stabbed so often that only the sockets remained, yet these two frightening hollows followed Amantu's every movement like gun barrels. All her toes had been lopped off long ago, her nose torn from her face, her breasts ripped out of her chest like turnips from a field. A hanging prune on either side of her head showed how the constant thrashing had torn off her impaled ears. The stump of her left arm waved about crazily, while the putrefied forearm and half-hand, still spiked to the cross's horizontal arm, hung at an angle, a withered black stem on a bone-yellow branch. Mama's right arm was intact to the mid-palm, where the fingers and meat of the hand had been ripped off in her frenzy, leaving only a gristly thumb. From this digit grew a foot-long curved yellow nail, chipped round the edges but with a tip sharp as a razor. Despite her unbelievable condition, the Mater Infector cackled gaily as her toothless old head rocked every which way, rattling the grinning black bogeyman beside her.

"Hammer!" Abel gasped, jarring the professor from his trance. "Over here, man! It's Ti! Give us a hand!"

Mama's head swung toward the sound and back to Amantu. She laughed hysterically while he backpedaled to his friends.

Mack's eyes were rolled way up, and he didn't appear to be breathing. His face and neck were a pox of cuts and contusions. "Grab his chest!" Abel grunted, squeezing around to raise a sprawled leg. Izzy took the other leg as Amantu, poised behind Mack, clasped his hands at the chest and strained to haul him upright. The man was a dead weight, the leverage all wrong. It took the Group three separate, protracted struggles to rock him into a standing slump. They walked him in a tight circle. With Amantu's back to *Cross*, Abel and Izzy lifted on Mack's legs. There was a giddy moment when the professor's body weight was the winning force, and it seemed they'd be able to stand the man straight. The next moment Amantu was staggering back under his own impetus, as though in slow motion. His startled expression matched those of his friends as they stood gaping, the unconscious astronomer propped between them.

A sharp pain ripped across the back of Amantu's neck. The Hammer whirled. Mama's sockets were fixed on him, her gummy jaw hanging. He snarled at that black empty mouth, and at the instrument that had sliced him—she was dangling her long curved thumbnail in his face, its stiletto tip gleaming with sputum and blood from her just-slit tongue—before his huge bull's knuckle of a fist slammed flush into her mangled Halloween face.

The impact doubled the frail old woman at the waist, shattering the cross and sending a hundred bone spurs through her back and out her belly. Her ecstatic death scream, echoing throughout the Heart and out into the adjacent tunnels and caves, was immediately answered by shrieks of unbearable envy. In an instant mobs of cripples were pouring into the chamber. The Group dragged Mack off the stage and slammed into a facing wall even as a dozen howling men leaped tooth and nail on the impaled corpse.

Only the shared body of Titus Mack kept the Group a group. They clung tenaciously, clearing a path along the tunnel's wall by elbowing, kicking, side-arming, and occasionally butting heads. Amantu, as backwards-striding front man, bore the brunt of the punishment. He held the position admirably, but was increasingly prone to bouts of faintness and confusion. The human flow thinned as it poured past. The Group found harbor in a wide hollow.

Amantu smacked against the rock back-first, slowly slid to his rear, and sat slumped with his head between his knees, still hanging onto Mack. Sweat poured off his nose and chin.

Abel rolled back an eyelid. "It's his heart, damn it. Entirely too much for him. We've got to rest."

The black head rose and fell. "No! Titus must be evacuated. I shall recover."

Izzy found the carotid with one hand and fanned the professor's face with the other. "He needs oxygen, Josh. This place is suffocating."

"I will be...right." Amantu, squeezing out from under Mack, forced himself erect by walking his spine up the wall. He slapped a hand to the back of his neck.

"No, Hammer," Abel said, "you will not. Not without adequate rest."

But the professor was already scooping Mack back up. "Later, Josh," he puffed. "Later."

Izzy and Abel exchanged glances, grabbed a limb a-piece, and swung their way out. Something subliminal in Mama's scream reverberated into the deepest tunnels, bringing armies of ravening rats up every passage. The monsters leapt on the thrashing cripples, driving their fangs into anything moist. The Group fought them back with torches, making their way against the stream on the theory that moving away from the Heart was moving toward an exit. The flow decreased steadily, and by the time they were stumbling alongside the tribe's cavern only the oldest and sickest rats were hobbling past, more confused than galvanized by all the excitement. Amantu's faltering progress made Mack's ill-distributed weight that much more cumbersome, and Izzy was at times a near-hysterical anchor. In the end their destination was determined solely by Abel's inspired guesswork, yet it was more luck than inspiration that brought the Group staggering up to Dan'l's Gate.

They conquered one step at a time, using their own sagging bodies to lever Mack to the top before kicking away the camouflage and collapsing as a unit on the stinking earth. Topside it was bright daylight; they could see the observatory like a white bubble in the distance. Abel shaded Mack with his body while checking vitals. He was a long while at it.

"AJ," gasped Amantu. "We must proceed. There is nothing we can do for him here." To make his point he resumed his position as lead man, raising Mack's torso from behind, preparing to stride in reverse. The men took their places and commenced half-carrying, half-dragging Mack. After a few yards Izzy threw on the brakes and dropped to his knees. A chill raced up Amantu's spine and he shuddered. A dozen cripples came swarming out of the spider hole, vanishing even as he shook his head. He wiped his eyes.

There was a yelp. Izzy lurched to his feet. "I'm up, damn you!"

Abel kicked him again. "Then *lift*, damn you." The three put their backs and hearts into it, awkwardly raising Mack a foot off the ground and stumbling along for thirty yards before staggering to a halt. Inch by inch the body dipped. When his rump touched the ground they all went down with him, Amantu keeping the body up in a sitting position.

"This," Abel gasped, "won't...*do!*"

"It *will* do," grunted Amantu. He turned on his knees until he was poised back-to-back, then ran his arms under Mack's. "It will *have* to do!" Throwing high his chin, he roared to his feet and began a resolute march.

"By the Mercies," Izzy gulped, "you, Hammer, are a man!" He grabbed one of Mack's trailing legs. Abel hoisted the other and Amantu lowered his head. Izzy and Abel ran across the Outs pushing the professor like a plow, steering him with side-to-side thrusts. Their grunts, at first syncopated, became synchronous and locomotive-like as they blindly pressed forward. Mack's head bounced and dangled, his frame swung side-to-side, his fingertips swept the dirt. As they picked up steam, each Group member in turn gave vent to a primal growl. Upon merging, the compound call rose in pitch and intensity until it was a sawing, full-throated howl of indomitable will. And the bubble became a blister, and the blister, a dome. And the Group slammed onto Mack's porch almost unknowing, burst through the wall, and collapsed in a heap on the soft gel floor.

Chapter Thirteen

Signature

For a while there, there were four dead men splayed out on the doctor's comfy round zodiac. Then, one by one, the bodies returned to life; listening to the room, pushing to their hands and knees.

"Brandy!" Izzy panted. "Administer. Quickly." He called up the liquor cabinet, wolfed down a portion, and juggled back a decanter. But no way could he make Mack drink. The doctor's mouth stood open at an angle. His cheeks were pallid and drawn. Abel ran the alcohol back and forth under Mack's gaping nostrils. "Salts!" he called out. "*Now!* Somebody check the lavatory! Anybody!"

Amantu wobbled across the room, pitched through the split skin, and slammed face-first into an indifferent neoprene partition. The back of his neck itched madly, his ears were ringing, nausea shook him in waves. Abel's voice stimulated a corresponding vibration in the intervening skin: "He's not breathing! *I can't find a pulse!* Hammer!"

Careening into the lavatory, Amantu was rocked by the train wreck of his reflection. He smashed the mirror aside, strewing the cabinet's contents. Scattered about the floor were tubes and bottles containing a variety of medications devoted almost exclusively to liver ailments, along with one vial clearly marked Ammonium Carbonate. Amantu took a whiff and the jolt did him good. He lunged back through the skin.

Abel shoved the vial under Mack's nose. "Now!" Izzy lifted and lowered the knees. Abel placed an ear on that wracked mouth. "Again!" Mack was wholly unresponsive, his eyes cloudy pools. Abel grimly launched into cardiopulmonary resuscitation while Izzy vigorously rubbed Mack's arms and legs. After a tense minute Abel sat back on his haunches and stared at the dying astronomer; filthy, near-naked, spread-eagled ignominiously, ragged skull strangled by a crude crown of hammered-in brambles. Burning resentment remade his expression. "Get him up. Get...him...*up!*"

It took everything Amantu had to haul Mack upright. Abel swung under an arm, Amantu supported the other, and together they dragged him around the room, trying to walk some life back into the man. Little by little their knees caved. Abel looked around wildly.

"Solo. Sign your runner." Mack was sagging. "For Christ's sake, *sign Titus Mack!*"

The body seemed to flicker gently between them, but even that impression was history by the time their knees hit the tiles.

"Cover," Izzy whispered. "Oh, man. Just cover him." In a minute he removed his own tattered outer robe and laid it tenderly over Mack's gnarled face.

The professor's eyes banged shut.

"*Hammer?*" Amantu jacked up his head. His friends were holding Mack half-off the floor, waiting. He took the legs this time, and they gently carried the body through the skin and onto the waiting bed. Izzy pulled a blanket over Mack's face, tucked a corner under his head.

The sense of loss, to Amantu, was oddly profound. Time ground to a halt. The temperature seemed to drop twenty degrees, and an electric silence filled the room. Abel leaned in close. "I'm so sorry, Ti. It's beyond wrong, beyond unfair. Why things are as they are—"

"Your work," Izzy told the blanket. "Your name. Carry on."

"Of course. We'll make Solomon the genius of your memory. Everybody will know you went out working."

Amantu felt Izzy's icy fingers on his own. He looked up. Across the bed, Abel was already holding Izzy's other hand. Amantu stuck out his big hot palm, completing the chain. All eyes were on him. The silence congealed.

"I do vow," the Hammer breathed, "to diligently honor the memory of my good friend Titus Mack."

The chain relaxed.

"Come," said Abel. "Let him have his peace."

The men filed out through the skin. Abel called up some seats. Amantu fell back, his arms dead at his sides. Izzy brought round the tray. When he reached the professor he said, "You look Hammer terrible. Afraid we insist." Abel nodded solemnly.

Sweet lava rolled down his throat. Marion Blackberry. Amantu could breathe again. He took another swallow.

"So," Izzy belched. He stared at his friends. "It behoove us. Be practical."

Abel's reply was heavy with the bitterness of fait accompli. "'Carry on.' Izzy, if it leaks we're onto an ugly massacre and cover-up, this place'll be stripped, sealed, and buried. History will remember Ti as an infected crackpot, and we three'll be quarantined as carriers. That's if they don't just shoot us first. No, Solomon's got to be kept a secret."

"*History*," Amantu heaved, "is all we have." He stood up.

Izzy set down his drink. "Hammer."

The professor said reasonably, "Solomon must be commanded to manifest the details of our past as they truly occurred. Whether or not the ramifications appeal." The brandy had done him good. He addressed the room as though from a lectern. "Our educable young, at least, deserve nothing less."

"Rot," said Abel. "You're delirious, man. Things have stabilized. You'll only upset four hundred years of successful adaptation."

"There you are mistaken, AJ. Sincere men will always make the most of truth. Our next step is bigger than us."

Abel rose. "Let it lie."

"Gentlemen," Amantu said grandly. He turned to the eastern skin. "Solo!"

On that prompt the dome blew off with a roar of geysers, spun whistling a half mile overhead, and collapsed on its foundation with a delicate *click*. Inrushing air compressed the room to a speck of white light. That light burst into an instantaneous nova, then into a zillion radiant spikes, and upon those spikes' dissolution the observatory's interior grew violently alive. The floor became the eye of a hurricane, the skin a furious display of rotating lights and shadows. Countless waveprint clusters hissed and flickered past, black squiggly schools of data tamped and dispersed like iron filings round a revolving magnet. And behind it all ran a disquieting th-*thud*, th-*thud*, th-*thud*, accelerating and retarding in perfect sync with the images. Oddly, Amantu's bullhorn of a voice could be heard off and on—words, grunts, sentence-fragments, popping out of the whirl before being blown to vocal shrapnel. With each demolished syllable the rushing imagery reacted correspondingly—spiderwebbing, exploding with spikes and troughs, sprouting filaments that vanished even as they formed.

Abel was reeling like a man on a merry-go-round. "Solo! For Christ's sake, *break!*" He caught his breath. "And please...whatever you do, don't anyone say anything that'll start him back up!"

"Something—" Amantu gasped. "Wrong. Something... terribly wrong."

Abel turned on him. "That was your voice, Hammer. I heard it."

"I uttered not a word!"

Izzy clamped his hands to his temples and folded at the waist. "O wracked and raging cerebrum—never again!" He took a deep breath and colored deeper. "I *mean* it this time!"

"Sure you do." Abel shook his head. "What a spectacle! The entire program's aborting! Ti must've written in a security release."

"He would not. As a man of science, he would deem Solomon's existence to be of far greater significance than his own. There is a glitch."

"Balls..." Izzy pulled himself together, "descending! But—we'll never learn by pitching praise and pity. I say, there! Solo!"

The skin shot round again, this time depicting an atomic shell swarming with electrons. Unrelated noises accompanied the phenomenon—rushing wind, electrical discharges, the sounds of surf. The swarm resolved, systematically, into rings, which merged, level by level, until the skin's smooth concave surface was again an opaque field. Apparent objects blew into being and disappeared; some merely planes and geometric shapes, some vaguely recognizable persons and contrivances. Through all this, Izzy's pipe of a voice phased in and out. A row of torches came streaming through the room, quickly followed by a rattle of gunfire and the sough of a breaching whale. A half moon shot across the upper skin.

"Solo! Break!"

"That..." sputtered Izzy, "was *me!* I'd know me anywhere."

"And there is our clue. First my voice, then the voice of Doctor Weaver here. The Solomon program is performing correctly by utilizing the voice of its runner. It responds to commands. But how does it verbalize independently?"

"Is Ti," Izzy said, blurting out the first thing that came to mind. "Is got to be."

"No!" Abel smacked the back of his friend's head. "But of course! We got to him in time! Solo!"

The room roared to life.

"Titus! It's Abel! Can you hear me?" Eerily, it was Abel's own voice that responded: *Abel!* Bas-relief patterns rocketed around the skin, grotesqueries mostly, moving way too fast to decipher. The voice repeated, *Abel*, and the room seemed to wobble. Facial features like sculpted soap bubbles popped in the air. There rang out a single syllable—*hold*—and the skin became a spinning carousel of body types interspersed with miscellaneous household objects. Blood-red tendrils, shooting into the center of the room, were immediately sucked back into the maelstrom.

"Solo! Break!"

"Those!" Izzy announced. "*Those!* Many fish—manna fist—manifes*ta*tions. Titus fight for program foothold while ...still try to make sense environment." Managing a huge breath, he articulated heroically: "It's a healthy response to stress. But comparable to madman—forgive colloquialism—to madman trying make sense reality." A second massive breath preceded an elegant conclusion: "Consciousness cannot compete with an encyclopedic environment! Just too much damned information."

Amantu was barely able to focus. "Then we must throw him a line."

Abel nodded. "Solo!"

A six-by-nine Abel-mask somersaulted halfway across the room before blowing into a billion bits. Other faces peeled off the skin and whipped about like bats.

"Memories!" Izzy shouted. "Mind seeking reestablish foundation!"

"Titus! Try to think in straightforward sentences, man. Think conversationally!"

A flurry of mental debris whisked around the room, compelling Abel to cup his mouth and yell, "*Signed*, Titus! You were signed by Solomon. The field's supporting your signature. Or vice-versa. Whatever. Your mind's engaged in real time. Or what used to be your mind. Christ, Ti—you were...you were *killed* by those lunatics out there! I can't believe I just said that."

The tempest skipped a beat. On restart, the room filled to the skin with a realistic impression of choking black smoke, and the Group were clinging like children as they plummeted toward a burning gray battleship on a gunmetal sea. An instant before impact, a series of splintering crashes rocked the north skin. The smoke cleared. Three men swinging double-edged axes burst in, took a quick look around, and ran straight through the Group into the skin's rapidly-adjusting phantom horizon.

Amantu swooned. By the time they got him on his feet they were back in the torch-lit Honeycomb Heart, watching dozens of painted men approach with stones in their fists and curled feet. The impression of an assault was eerily realistic; the Group instinctively turned to see what these predators were stalking, only to find dozens more seemingly closing in from behind. When they turned back they found those projected human spiders in the act of hurling their stones with malicious intent. With the barrage mere inches away, the program shifted to a massive glacial calving, complete with titanic roar and explosive impact. A second later the Group were on an unfamiliar battleground amidst countless butchered men. Digitized wind moaned over the tragedy like a bereaved old woman. The room took off again.

"Reliving!" Izzy shouted. "Sperience! Mix with random—with tandem...that was *Colony!*"

"He's not even alive, you idiot. And *nobody's* lived all that. You are *so* drunk. Solo. Break."

Amantu interjected. "You are both correct." All he wanted was to curl up and die. "In appearance, Ti's signature is attaching and detaching haphazardly. Evidently it is one thing to run this program, and quite another to run *in* it." His eyes grew heavier as he spoke. The hot lids kissed, and he might have passed out on his feet, if not for a projected, gut-wrenching wail of mass supplication. His eyes popped back open.

It was night again, and the Group were standing elbow-to-elbow in a crowd stretching as far as the program could handle. A thousand generator-driven searchlights probed the earth and heavens; some fixed on the wide black sky, some dancing their beams laterally to goad the crowd. Half a mile to the west lay a carousel-like ring of these bright columnar beams, dedicated to a wheeled platform stacked high with speaker towers and tiered racks of amplifiers. Numberless men and women stood close enough to chafe, mesmerized by that white-hot spot.

Then, in a wild, hallucinatory break from reality, the nearest individuals whirled and stared directly at the Group. The action was repeated by a second ring, and another and another, the effect spreading smoothly and dramatically like ripples breaking up a pond. Within seconds every face in the place was gaping, and every voice within immediate earshot had been stilled. No experience could have been more unnerving; the Group, instinctively standing back-to-back, were receiving the same impression from all sides: endless startled expressions, countless hanging jaws, and two seconds later they were bombarded by searchlight beams. The men were more stunned than blinded—these beams, mere projections, were being reproduced at a candlepower that could not exceed Solomon's partitioned output.

"Solo! Break!"

Throats were cleared, fists unclenched. At last Izzy muttered, "Funniest thing. Just had...dream. Strange. Standing there, big old crowd, everybody yelling, hooting. Alla sudden they just turn and...*stare* at me."

Abel raised an eyebrow. "Can dreams be shared? How about you, Hammer?" But Amantu was still a deer in headlights. Abel nodded. "Okay then. There we were, backed up against one another. Let's try it again." When they were satisfactorily aligned, Abel said, "Solo. Repeat Last Sequence. Real Time."

Again it was night. Again the Group were swallowed up in that unbelievable throng, again the nearest individuals turned to stare, again the ripple effect took place.

"Solo. Stop."

Abel had paused the playback with perhaps half the observable crowd staring in astonishment and the rest captured in various stages of just catching on. He said, very clearly, "Ti, old friend...Titus, if you can hear me...you are—you were a thinking man. So you'll forgive me if I tweak you a bit here, just a little. Solo. Zoom in and Mark. Enlarge by ten."

As the projections' dimensions expanded tenfold, Solomon's feathered pixilation produced images with overlapping patches of varying opacity. Butcher's frozen followers were now splotchy see-through colossi, looking over the Group's heads with expressions of intense surprise. From this vantage, the inner ring of filmy giants appeared to be trading stares with opposing individuals. At the ring's dead-center, the relatively tiny real men turned about in unison, following those stares, until they found themselves facing one another, profoundly confused and embarrassed.

"Solo," Abel said. "Return to Mark." The giants zoomed back to normal size and profusion.

"Maybe I get it," Abel muttered, "and maybe I don't. Earlier we were watching these visuals stare at Ti's anomaly— and now they're checking us out." He studied the life-sized figures carefully. No doubt about it; they were looking right at, and right through, the closely huddled Group. "I guess I don't get it."

Izzy peered up blearily. "Not us, '*idiot*.' We not there! We...here. They look at Ti."

Abel smacked him again. "Thirty years you wait to say something brilliant. And now: twice in one night!"

Izzy colored. "Well, I...sometime in brainstudy find—"

"Solo," Abel said. "Break." The house lights came back up. "Tsunami," he mused. "A billion deluded sheep, all braying in concert." He faced the southern skin, trying to remember verbatim while winging it. "'Oh Soul of the burning night. Oh Soul, oh-*Soul*, oh...*Soul*oh—'" And the room roared to life. "Break." The lights came back up. He turned to Izzy. "Okay, skullcracker. Tell us how a disembodied dead man is able to leap four hundred years into the past."

Amantu pulled himself together. "Gentlemen. We are obviously pioneering an esoteric branch of physics here. We all know that time does not exist as a medium. These are haphazard attachments. Ti's signature is hopping about electromagnetically, independent of our continuum notions. It is no wonder Butcher's followers reacted so dramatically. Given the physical similarity to their executed hero, they sincerely believed they were witnessing the manifestation of their divinity." He raised his leaden arms to demonstrate. "Poor Titus was signed even as we attempted to walk him around this room."

"Genius!" Abel marveled. "I'm surrounded by genius!"

Izzy rolled up his head. "Well, I—"

"Solo!" The whirl started up. "*Titus!*" The world went dark, save for the glow of a single sputtering candle in a dirty black cave. Facing away, Samuel Butcher knelt in genuflection, his head bowed and his hands clasped. Suddenly aware of the signature behind him, he jerked round and looked up at the Group guiltily, gave a little yelp, and collapsed on his face. He lay there with his chin in the rocks as though a heel were planted on the back of his neck. The visual accelerated. Night and day popped in and out in a dizzying stream, producing all the symptoms of vertigo. Amantu embraced his stomach and doubled over.

"Damn it all, Hammer!" Abel's voice was out of a dream. "Izzy, unhand that brandy. Get some damp towels from the lavatory, and while you're at it check for nitroglycerine." Amantu felt liquid dribbling between his lips. "I'm afraid it's the real thing this time." The dirty gold robes were ripped down to his navel. An ear pressed against his chest.

Down and drifting, Amantu watched storm clouds racing across the upper skin. Part of him wanted to tell Abel that his heart wasn't the problem, but another part told him to play it the way it looked. Artificial night and day continued to darken and brighten the room, along with that peculiar flicker produced by torches. And now a lumbering body, as large as the observatory, paused mid-stride, filling the entire chamber with the dingy mist of its projected shadow. In the next breath the men were to all appearances stepped on by a brontosaur. Amantu sat up and shook his head. "Solo. Stop."

The place had turned into a cretaceous greenhouse crammed with fern twenty feet high. Swamp gas pixel-clouds hung on the projected horizon like tossed pepper. The professor struggled to his feet as the scene skipped off, becoming, in quick succession, a submarine valley, some kind of celebration in an outdoor stadium, and an open-ended vista of stellar space. "So—" He tried again. "Solo! *Stop!*" And the men stood suspended high above the planet, staring out at a luminous young solar system. Dust and planetesimals were caught in the act of accumulating, backlit by a frozen blond ball. The grandeur and raw beauty were just too much. All life left Amantu's legs, and he sagged into his friends' embrace.

Abel hauled him upright. "How's that for history, Professor? Nothing but grit and gas." His voice was sandpaper on Amantu's eardrum. "But it goes back farther, Hammer. It has to. Do you want to see? How's about you, Izzy? What do you say, guys? Let's go all the way to inception." He took Izzy's right hand and the professor's left. Izzy completed the ring. "Open your mind, Hammer, and don't be afraid. We've got you, man. And we're not letting go."

What happened next might have been one more detail in Amantu's delirium. Mack's house lights shot up, rudely replacing the majestic stellar projection with that familiar old world of blank white skin and gel motif. The Group broke hands and turned, expecting to find another incursion of rabid Colonists.

In the skin's wide breach stood a small mob in civilian clothes, military uniforms, and bright orange hazards suits. Between bodies could be seen slices of a special forces cavalcade. A dozen men in bulky protective gear jogged to within a few yards of the Group, went into genuflection left-to-right, and leveled their firearms. When the last man's knees hit the floor, eight simultaneous pulses, four for each man, blew Abel and Izzy off their feet in a gale of gore and body parts.

Amantu's jaw dropped, a spittle bubble forming between his gaping lips. There was blood everywhere. He stared back at the line of gunmen in dead silence. The bubble grew; it seemed every trigger finger was just waiting on it. The professor went limp. His heart almost stopped when the bubble popped.

Chapter Fourteen

Closure

"Okay," called a voice in the back. "Everybody stand down. Those bodies are not to be touched by anyone."

A man in casual wear walked to the line of executioners, looked Amantu directly in the eyes, and smiled warmly. Without looking away, he dropped his arms in a chopping motion and barked, "Lower those weapons immediately! You men move out and return to your stations!" Then, in a voice almost tender, "I'd like a moment alone with the professor." When the room was clear he snapped on a transparent mask and worked his arms into a pair of elbow-length surgical gloves.

"Moses Matthew Amantu! How I've longed to meet you!" The mask fogged slightly at the cheeks. "You'll forgive me for not shaking hands. Strictest orders. My name's Thomas Ryder—but please feel free to call me Tommy. And there's something so distant about the term 'Mister,' don't you think? Anyways, sorry about all the mess. Damned cops. But what're you gonna do?" He glanced at the mangled bodies with distaste. "Well. I'm what's known in the Barrier's M Section as a Closer. Occasionally citizens get caught up in police-style actions, entitling them to financial reparation, to legal assistance, to professional counseling and—generally their first concern—to an immediate explanation." He lowered his head while raising his eyes. "Ah, sir! Such a time you've had! Do take a seat. And allow me to fix you a drink."

Amantu didn't budge. His diseased old heart was beating far too hard, yet he'd never been more aware of being alive. "Thank you, no. And I prefer to remain standing. You mentioned an explanation."

"Of course." The Closer crimped his nose. "But please, not here. Not with the dead." He swept an arm. "I'm afraid I must insist."

The professor, swooning, backpedaled until his shoulders met the bespattered skin.

Ryder nodded crisply. "So be it." He pursed his lips and, his eyes twinkling behind the mask's glass, stepped right past. The skin breached, but remained open after he'd passed through. Amantu looked everywhere but down, fighting to control his breathing while the Closer checked on Mack's body.

A few minutes later Ryder sauntered back in, shaking his head and wiping down his gloves. "I had no idea carriers beat the crap out of their assimilators before they died." He scrolled down his pocket scrambler. The men in protective suits, accompanied by forensics officers holding prongs and scanners, lumbered back in dragging sterilized body bags. The Closer jerked a thumb at Mack's bedroom.

"Just *what*—" Amantu gasped, "just what do you *mean* by that?"

Ryder turned back. "I mean you've been taken for a ride, my friend, both figuratively and literally. These messy specimens, along with that beat-up and diapered individual in the bedroom—all the members of this so-called 'Group,' in fact—were snatchers. They were Colony agents."

Amantu pushed himself to his full height. Half a head taller than Ryder, he snarled down with all the righteousness he could muster, "And *you*, sir, are an outright liar! Good men have been murdered—friends of mine. Who *are* you people?" He was hyperventilating. "I thought this day had seen the last of lunatics and highwaymen."

The Closer's mask fogged again. "Think back, Professor. Not too far—to just shortly after midnight. Do you remember entertaining a stranger between the hours of oh-one twenty-four and oh-one forty-seven? A telepresence utilizing a stolen police scrambler dropped in on you and the gang as you merrily crossed the Burghs to meet the new year. Well, that Tp was in actuality a Colony agent, working in the guise of a gnarly street hustler. He was not a very good agent. He was only supposed to provide a certain psychotropic substance, not introduce a loaded military weapon. A Medium Range Assault arm was fired on that View, resulting in the near-instantaneous apprehension of said agent directly at the projection site. Our association proved most amenable. Over the course of half an hour he provided a wealth of insight into the Colony's machinery; names, posts—things we hadn't the foggiest idea about. The man swore he'd spill the undreamable if only we'd let him live." Ryder's eyes warmed with secret amusement. He shrugged. "Odds are long he will.

"Now, everything I'm relating came straight from him, and it's all been verified by creatively squeezing half a dozen federally-housed carriers prized for their compliance under questioning. Now try to remember, Professor. *Did* that Tp import a controlled substance onto that View ride?"

Amantu sagged. "Only a mild stimulant. Of what possible legal consequence—I have—I have this heart condition."

"And I'm sure it's a good one. You were lucky your pals were there. They saved you from indulging…?"

"They did not. It was their common effort to revitalize me. They may have saved my life." It struck him. "They most certainly saved my life! They were professional men. I trusted them; in their zeal, their capableness."

"A good call. Most Colony agents are every bit as qualified as their civil counterparts. Plus, they're provided top-notch intelligence. Knowing your cardiac patterns, a member was assigned to provoke a case of angina, and another to convince you to indulge in a restorative tonic. At the appropriate moment, one of your new pals signaled the projecting agent by faking an emergency call. According to our little squealer, the assigned concoction contained a street drug known as Swirl, mixed with an Eastern synthetic capable of producing hallucinations ranging from paranoid to euphoric over a twelve-hour period. You've been slipped a dream, Professor.

"Now, one of Swirl's more-popular effects is its ability to open up even the toughest nut: susceptibility to suggestion, libidinous fantasies, a glorious sense of brotherly love. Users become wide-open to new ideas."

"Sober intellectuals are always open to new ideas."

"Oh, come on, Amantu! We know all about you and your steel-trap brain. You've never heard a word you didn't want to hear, and your fondest displays of acknowledgement are grunts and truncated scowls. Given that, it was the job of these snatchers to win you over: to win your focus, your trust, your affection—no mean feat. Yet here you are, still with 'em. Not such a standoffish guy after all."

Amantu pondered the Group's faces; not those gory distorted outrages smeared across the gel's Pisces, but the very personal, if at times galling, countenances still fresh in memory. He heard again their jibes, their insights, their petty outbursts. These had been real people. They'd done right by him. Tommy Ryder was, by contrast, an arrogant bully with a very big bureaucratic bug up his butt.

"You'd been suitably prepped. The next step was to get you here for further inducement."

"What 'further inducement'?"

"You were to be treated to a feast for the eyes and imagination, something no *historian*"—and he spat the word—"could resist. According to our canary, this riveting spectacle involved a lost art utilizing what he referred to as '*dancey lights*'." Ryder's eyes took in every detail of the skin and floor. "Looks pretty tame to me. So what did our good doctor do, lecture ad infinitum? How quaint." He rolled his neck. "Once you'd been induced, your new buddies were to bring you into the Colony for infection and assimilation. Does any of this sound famil—" Ryder cut himself short, raising a hand and backing off as Mack's body was rolled out in a transparent cocoon. When the specialists were out of earshot he upped the ugliness in his tone.

"Here's something you can teach your students, pal. Titus Mack was the Burghs' Head Assimilator. Who knows how many decent citizens his boys snaught? Who knows how many he prepped, in this very toilet, for said infection and assimilation? Makes my stomach crawl. How's 'bout yours?" Ryder's expression behind the glass was that of a man probing a clogged drainpipe. "Why do you think he lived all the way out here, anyway?"

"He was," Amantu wheezed, "a man of research. Great men need great privacy."

"Come again? Great actor is more like it. Mack kept up his healthful front like all gifted carriers—through sheer will. Only the riffraff run around raving and biting each other. But Titus Mack was a Y-Class with terminal liver disease. The Colony needed a new man for the site, and he was thoughtful enough to volunteer your name. Nudge, nudge, Amantu: How coincidental that your work in recall should fall right in line with the Colony's overall strategy."

"Not another word! You did not know these fine men. They were *thinking* individuals, not reactive ones. Seekers of truth, not fabrication."

They parted for the forensics crew. The Closer oversaw the entire affair with crisp efficiency; an important man accustomed to having his orders followed precisely. Izzy's and Abel's bits and pieces were systematically tagged, bagged, and sealed. The professor clung to consciousness while one crew scanned the premises and another cleaned up. The skin and floor were scrubbed meticulously. By the time the workers had departed, every trace of the lives and deaths of three men had departed with them. The skin hissed shut. The observatory was now a ghost house, but still ringing with the memories of miscellaneous commands. The whole process had taken perhaps twenty minutes, yet Ryder was able to pick up the conversation as though no interruption had occurred:

"Big on truth, were they? These guys were Method masters, pros from the word go. They had you eating right out of their hands. And, speaking of hands, you been holding any lately? Joining any 'circles' or 'rings?' By the look of things, you were cozying right up when we busted in here. 'Not snaught for naught,' eh, Professor? Well, let me throw something else at you, Mr. Thinking Man. I'll just bet that this wonderful Titus Mack of yours told you some sad story about a bunch of religious nuts who were incinerated in a great big cave a long time ago, right? And maybe he added that it was the government's fault, so they covered it up by calling it mass suicide, and wrote it into history that way. No! Wait a minute. I'm gonna go *way* out on a limb here. I'm gonna guess he told you that their supernatural creator showed up, and that the government didn't want anybody to know about *that* either. I've heard umpteen variations on the story, from every carrier sick enough to jabber his way into custody." Ryder screwed up his expression and clenched his fists melodramatically.

"*Damn* it all, Amantu, I'm gonna go way, *way* out—to the very tip of that limb! I'm gonna posit that Mack even 'showed' you this supernatural whatchamacallit; this 'God,' this glowing guy on a stick—that he *proved* it to you. I wish I could have been here for that one, man. I'll bet you're downright *positive* you've seen this thing." He called up a draped-and-tagged gel couch, then made a pretense of peeking behind it. "How's about you show it to me? Then we can both pull out the whips and razors. And you won't even have to take me all the way out to see your Madame Rat—you can prick me right here, prick. I'm one of the dumb ones." He called the couch back down.

"How *dare* you! Just what are you implying?"

"I'm trying to say you're a carrier, Amantu."

"Liar! Liar! *Liar!* You have produced nothing *but* lies! From the moment your murderous circus violated this venerated place of research." The skin breached. A small phalanx of medical personnel made their way in. A couple of nurses at the fore zipped themselves into transparent body stockings, activated their masks, and stepped up wielding long plastic-tipped tongs.

"Aw, c'mon, Prof'! No need to get personal. But tell me; how you been feeling lately, huh? A little faint? A bit under the weather? Nausea, maybe, or flashes and sweats? How about hallucinations? I've heard it's one hell of a ride at the onset of contraction. Think of it! Without an inkling, you were drugged, snaught, and infected—you've been all but crowned! Yet you claim to know what's real and what's not. How dare *you!*"

Amantu was hit with a tranquilizer. In seconds his arms and legs were made of wood, his head stuffed with cotton. A doctor scanned his optics and an assistant cut off his filthy gold robes with sterile scissors. Nurses picked up the rags with pneumatic pincers and dropped the mess into a large see-through pouch. They draped him in a cellophane hospital gown, stuffed his bloody feet in a pair of padded slippers, and stapled a radio ID bracelet to his wrist. The nurses stepped back. Amantu was hit with a stimulant. The medical personnel picked up their gear and filed back out the skin. Amantu forced out his words.

"Why then—why—why was I not also dispatched? After all you have related...you expect me to believe...you would leave a carrier here to—to carry on such despicable work? Why not put *me* out of *my* misery?"

The Closer wagged his head regretfully. "Sorry, not an option: I don't make those decisions in the field. Everything's been figured out. No 'despicable work' will be done here, for the simple reason that the jig is up on this place. Your masters will learn, soon enough, that their scheme has backfired. But don't you worry about 'em taking it out on you, Mosey. They wouldn't think of harming one of their own." Ryder backpedaled slowly, pausing every third step to mark his points. "*We* don't want you to suffer either, okay? As Mack's old colleague, you should appear happily engrossed in your vital recall work; freed from the burthen of students and faculty, able to transmit your findings directly to our offices for campus distribution. We want you to live long, healthily, and in complete security. You see, here you are much more valuable alive than dead. And so here you shall remain. You may, sir, consider yourself under permanent house arrest." The Closer blurred as he receded.

"Why—" Amantu gasped, fighting for cohesive breath, "—if what you say is truth, why should these poor people be sequestered generation after generation, locked away from the birthright of civilization? Why would a disease rage cureless *for over four centuries?* And why should plague data remain classified in the first place?" His head fell. "What is it my government does not want me to know?"

Ryder stopped where he was. He carefully modulated his voice, speaking with the succinctness of a bully explaining the new ground rules.

"Now pay close attention, 'Hammer.' Your government wants you to know that, as a vector, you're quarantined here on a permanent basis. Your government wants you to know that, as its beneficiary, you'll earn your keep by serving as its newest propaganda tool; video presentations, starring you, will be doctored to produce recall data amenable to right-thinking. Your government also wants you to know that, as your sponsor, it guarantees to provide for you throughout an extensive and highly productive tenure.

"And lastly, Amantu, your government wants you to know that Barrier members, as one of the hardest and fastest rules in nature, *do not* like carriers, *do not* like plague sympathizers, and most definitely *do not* like intellectual busybodies, especially of the 'historian' ilk." At the skin Ryder lifted his mask to flash a smile. "Don't bother," he said, leaning back until the new breach met his contours. "I'll let myself out." Behind him was dirty bright daylight. A perimeter had already been established, complete with police line, scads of official vehicles, and a mobile lab for the forensics specialists. The Closer stepped onto the porch and the skin's lips kissed shut. The observatory's interior dimmed steadily.

Amantu rested until he'd gathered the strength to push himself off. When he could get his mouth together he whispered, "Solo!"

The room dimmed further. A ghostly cocoon formed about the professor, glowing softly.

"Release all security blocks. Titus! M Section has control of your property! AJ and Izzy have been shot dead, implicated in some official insanity about a carrier conspiracy. I have been infected in the Colony, and without remedy will soon collapse. Instruct Solomon to scan my physical self so as to identify the pathogen."

The slowly swirling nebula vanished. Amantu's bleary eyes hung like pendants in the dark.

"Solo. Text Alone, Free-standing. Titus! I have in some manner been set up. I am a prisoner, at my wit's end. Explain what is going on."

The anticipated hovering text did not appear. It came to Amantu on a chill: the program wouldn't accept an unkeyed 'Titus' link. It took an extra measure of courage to pursue the obvious.

"Solo. Am I mad?"

Cold white light brushed his eyes. A photographic

image of nil value winked and was gone. In the ensuing fade-to-black Amantu spoke with exaggerated care.

"So-lo. Scan…my…physical…self. Describe *anything* awry—nervous, enzymatic, organic—anything that might result in a state of altered perception."

Amantu's insides were revealed in splendid detail. Pulmonary and respiratory organs, vividly active, blushed scarlet. Nerves, sinews, and cartilaginous bodies were etched in beautifully-highlighted cobalt on pearl.

The room went dark.

Amantu's white floating eyes fixed on the residual glow. "Solo! Text Alone!" He beetled his brows. "Have I ingested, accidentally or through a second party, any substance capable of affecting my senses or cognitive processes?"

A snapshot and blackness.

"Solo! Produce a catalyst! Search your files for *any* agent that might induce hallucinations in an otherwise healthy individual!"

A heartbeat later, eight misty blocks were hovering at eye-level, two feet away. The word

HYPNOSIS

was a new one. Amantu tried it out phonetically.

"Hype…no…sis. Solo. A brief description."

HYPNOSIS
NOUN> SLEEP-LIKE STATE
INDUCED BY A SECOND PARTY
SECONDARY NOUN>HYPNOTISM

"Hype…*no*-tism," Amantu tried. "*Hype*-notism…" He dropped his eyes. Barely able to stand, he mumbled, "Oh, Solo. What manner of man would do such a thing?"

The Text response was instantaneous.

HYPNOTIST

Amantu's eyes flashed like a tiger's.

"Hypenotist!"

He stomped through the room, calling up and smashing all things Mack.

"Hypnotist—*Fool!* Hypnotist—Rube! 'Dancey lights!' Ah! I am a pawn! A patsy! A puppet played by a master!"

A blast of hot air almost knocked him over. Overwrought and vertiginous, he gripped the breached skin's lips and snapped back his head.

In broad daylight, the Outskirts was the same wide-open dump he'd first seen by a drifting new year's moon. The porch was vacant, the horizon blank, the ground devoid of fresh tracks and prints. He knuckled his eyes and loped across the porch, but the moment he violated the perimeter his ID bracelet came alive and his errant foot received a jangling thrill. It wasn't all that bad, so he tried again, boldly extending an entire leg. And that time it hurt. Amantu stepped back, tugging on the tightening bracelet. He wasn't going anywhere.

Shrinking into his slippers and gown, Amantu wheezed and shuffled back inside. The old Mack place was palpably vacant, as quiet as a morgue. Dirty plates and untensils, unwashed robes, orthopedic furniture, dusted-over equipment and piled peripherals. The Hammer pulled his hospital gown tighter and, standing in the utter darkness of ignorance, whispered, *"Solo?"*

━━━━━━━━━━━━━━━━━━━━━━━━━━━━━━━━━

"And so," the old man said, "for upwards of eleven decades I have labored here, patiently attempting to establish some sort of permanent contact with Titus Mack. I have been only marginally successful. You see, the Solomon program was self-written with Titus as runner. A two-way window will require Solomon's adoption of my every idiosyncrasy…and I will confess to periods of wool-gathering." He auto-descended to near eye-level. "Yet, by dint of a most resolute nature, I have succeeded in producing a free-floating, rude shadow of the original field. This minor feat was accomplished by following the great astronomer's instructions through a kind of digitized Morse we wrote together, diaphragmatically assisted by Solomon himself.

The resulting medium, a wave-sensitive field contained in a battery-powered vacuum jar, was named '*Gist*' by Solomon. We felt he reserved that right of christening, for Ti and I could not have done it without him. After all, as Titus says, the Gist is 'Solomon's baby.'

"Now, it is urgently essential that you get this Gist into the hands of a man of science; a man able to complete the job. I have not been allowed a guest, nor been permitted to leave these premises, for some hundred-plus years—even though all rumors of plague are eradicated, even though civilization swept over this poor workhorse long ago, even though the Outskirts are little more than a dirty memory.

"You there: child! Your forefinger should be raised in a display of rhapsodic comprehension, not nastily thrust up a distended nostril. It behooves all mankind that my words are well-marked, so pay scrupulous attention. Follow me: the Gist is analogous to a man with spinal column damage. The will is there, but the nervous bridge is down. Contact must not be long-curtailed or the field will dissipate! Ti *must* be prodded!"

The children stared back and forth, their expressions ranging from mooning innocence to barely suppressed hilarity. A few mimicked old Amantu's puffy cheeks and bulbous eyes, others pantomimed a supine walrus in freefall. These physical impersonations, for all their overblown outlandishness, were fairly accurate—Moses Amantu's condition was wide open to the rudest form of mockery. At one hundred and seventy-four years of age he'd more than doubled his natural lifespan, and was now paying dearly for the dubious gift of artificially-induced longevity. He weighed four hundred and seventeen pounds, thirty-one ounces and eight grams; his body fat was stabilized at an even eighty-seven percent. The children were aware of this, as it was very clearly delineated on the frame's liquid crystal display. What they didn't know was that every gram of that lolling bulk had to be buoyed by a gyro-operated mattress consisting of thousands of tiny stress-responsive padded pistons, or his body would simply roll off its hovering "Crib" and plop onto the porch like a tubful of gelatin. Amantu's blood-engorged eyes had the same problem: without the spongy cupped wings that made up the rims of his lensless goggle-like glasses, the aqueous old orbs would slide right out of their sockets at the least concussion. That sculpted pillow supporting his soft wide skull was really a padded compartment for an oxygen cylinder. A pair of slender tubes, one emerging from each side of this pillow, bent round his massive old head and clipped onto a nose-shaped plate attached to the goggles. Out of sight, the tubes were sutured into nasal passages. The litter's chassis contained computer-driven micro-devices for supporting every vital function of the 15th Century's seniors, all ergonomically designed, all artfully secreted.

Now the pumps worked overtime, compensating for a brief surge of passion as Amantu aimed the Crib at his audience and spewed, "You *must*—you must *very* carefully preserve this Gist, or..." he gasped, "or..."

"Or what?" said that young smart aleck Boone, much to the delight of his little buddies. "You'll pee all over us?" Half a dozen scattered like chickens, shrieking with hilarity.

Sensors in the Crib's armrests immediately picked up on the Hammer's spiking blood pressure, stimulating a near-instantaneous firing of *Axxons*® in precise response to every nerve impulse in his left forearm. The hovering Crib swung, with digitally-controlled outrage: toes down, left-bearing. Warning lights ran round the litter and dimmed: old Amantu's moment of anger had cross-kicked his adrenals. Just framing a suitable retort left him silent and spent.

The knobby little bigmouth tossed his head at the gaping Callum twins.

"C'mon! Let's *go*. Let's let the old frog-man croak in private." He grabbed Darla Maker's hand as though she were a leashed dog, picked up his skimmer, and whirled it across the yard. Before the Callums could respond, Boone was running like a quarterback, still holding Darla. He swung her as he leapt, catching her waist in the same move so that the two landed photogenically on the whipping skimmer's static hub. Boone leaned her forward. Amantu watched resentfully as the cheering twins jumped off the porch and went bounding through the flagging overgrowth.

A stirring to his left triggered sensors in the goggles. A-mantu rolled his eyes. The Crib turned, dipping slightly in response to pressure from his left elbow.

It was that damned Archer boy—the blond pauper's son with the rebuilt hip and femur. That execrable prosthesis whirred and ratcheted for the zillionth time as the child, having enviously watched his friends once again dash off without him, nervously gimped back around. Amantu had never liked the boy; he was slow and hollow-eyed. His silent unbroken stares were ruder, somehow, than the daily derision of that whole receding pack of snot-noses. The boy's primitive, poor man's prosthesis didn't endear him either. The noise grated: *Hwee*, thump. *Hwee*, thump. Again and again. Over and over. And over and over and over and over and Amantu harumphed tinnily. Before he could draw another blank, he addressed his favorite imaginary audience, in the process forgetting all about little Archer. "It is intellectually difficult to accept, on the one hand, that Titus Mack is indeed God-becoming—not in an omnipotent sense, of course, but in the wise of omniscience. On the other hand, he *is* the mind of the universe in potential; existing as a part of all things that *have occurred* on our little sphere, and as a part of all things that *are occurring* in real time. He is, to all indications, alive, alert, and vigorous. But without mantle. As a non-corporeal entity, Mack cannot feel, cannot suffer, cannot perish—and this gives him freedoms foreign to structured being. He speaks excitedly, in that rough but ever-developing code of ours, of eventually attenuating by attaching to starlight, and so forever disencumbering himself of our planet's gravitational pull." Amantu sighed wispily. The effort almost stalled him.

His eye caught a hovering speck on the horizon. Amantu paled, and the machinery accelerated fractionally. "Demolition," he managed. A second later the Crib's sensors were all over the place. The nose-plate fogged. "Get underneath!" he gasped. "Place your hands on the rails." Once the boy had complied, Amantu banked the Crib hard to lee. The skin breached and they wobbled inside. House lights waxed serenely as the skin kissed closed behind them.

Amantu laboriously steered the Crib until it was hovering a few feet above the squashed couch by the dilapidated southern skin. "On that stand," he hissed. "Underneath the black cloth…a bell jar. Fetch it here, and be exceedingly mindful as you do so." Archer very carefully limped over to the stand, lifted the jar as if it were a Ming vase, and very carefully limped back to Amantu's Crib. "Set it, with the utmost delicacy, upon this little table."

Archer did so. Amantu tightened his grip on the armrest, activating a chrome pincers on a telescoping arm. As the old man gently rocked his palm on the rest, the pincers responded by just as gently oscillating above the cloth. He closed his fingers and elevated his wrist. The pincers plucked the cloth off the jar, dragged it down one side, and dropped it on the table.

Inside was two liters of empty space. The jar was airtight and rounded at the top, with a two-inch armored base containing a short stack of disk-shaped atomic batteries. Positioned on one side, just where the wall sloped into the cap, was a black vulcanized diaphragm about the size of a man's palm.

"Upon that diaphragm," Amantu wheezed, "one places one's lips when addressing the Gist. The Gist can only be activated by the spoken command '*Solo*'."

At the name the jar's interior appeared to sparkle slightly. Archer dropped to his good knee, his expression rapt. "Fairy dust!" When he looked back up, Amantu's face and hands were the color of tallow. The Crib dropped against the couch, autocorrected, and resumed hovering at an awkward angle. Archer rose hesitantly, trying to keep his fake leg from squealing. He watched the purple lips writhe.

"Boy…boy…that nickname—the unique vibrations produced by those two precisely articulated syllables—is a password. Those wavelengths act as a key to open the Solomon program through his Gist. You must find an adult…repeat to him what I have told you. Explain what is at stake for mankind—no, no—tell him to bring the Gist to men of science. At the university they will pick up where I have left off. But you must remember the password! Tell the science men to use it." An ice-blue moan rolled out of Amantu's depths. His head would have fallen to the side had not the equipment autoadjusted. With the last of his strength, he willed the Crib to face Archer directly.

"Cover it," he coughed. "Put it under your coat. Keep it

out of the light. Under no circumstances must a seal be broken—the Gist *must not* be exposed to air!"

Archer obediently pulled the cloth back over the jar and
tucked it under his raggedy overcoat.

"Now go."

The boy hesitated. "But what about you, sir? I—I can't
leave you here."

"Be gone, boy! And do not look back. Your work is
ahead of you."

Archer sniffled to the skin. As it splayed to meet him he
looked back, momentarily blinded by daylight. "But I don't
want to go, sir. I want to stay here with you."

A faint snarl. "I said get out! Do as you are told!"

Archer looked down at his plastic foot. "But I *want* to
stay," he sniffed. "I—I want to be here with *you*, sir."

A series of ugly wet grunts. Archer kept his eyes glued
to the tiles. In a minute that faltering old voice whispered back,
"But I do not want to be with *you*, you filthy little cripple. I
have always despised you. Always! Do as you are told! Get out
of my house, get out of my life. Get out of my sight!"

Archer unsuccessfully fought his tears. "Sir—"

"*Cripple!*"

A couple of splats preceded a high steady whine. The
Crib hissed to the floor.

Archer hobbled down the observatory's overgrown dirt
path, holding the Gist tightly under his coat. Unable to think
past his tears, he came upon the road unawares. A whisking
sound cut right in front of him and a blow to the ear almost
knocked him down. He carefully balanced the jar against his
chest and looked up.

Boone kept a hard eye on him as he helped Darla off his
skimmer; a gentleman leading a lady from her coach. When she
was on solid ground he strutted up, his expression fierce.
"Gimme your bottle, Archie. C'mon! I know the old frog give it
to you. Gimme that damn bubble-boogie!"

Archer bent deep at the waist while Boone whaled on
him. There was a smacking sound followed by a very unmanly
squeal. Still shielding the Gist, Archer peeked between his
crossed wrists. Darla was standing in front of the assailant with

one hand raised. By the stunned look on the boy's face it was obvious he'd just been slapped, and slapped *hard*. When he could face her again, he did so with only one welling eye.

The girl was on fire. "You leave him be; he's not hurting anybody! Let him keep his silly bottle." She stormed back to the skimmer. Boone whirled, the eye now streaming.

"Listen. You didn't see nothing. *Okay?* Nothing! You blab and I'll break off that phony leg of yours and stuff it down your throat foot-first. You got me?"

Archer lowered his head and waited for the next barrage. After a few seconds Boone turned and hurled the skimmer rowdily. It was a good spin, nearly horizontal and right on the money. He and Darla jumped on in tandem, and as they pressed their bodies forward the skimmer fairly leaped along the road. The girl had just time to peer back, throwing Archer a look that would bother him well into his teens. He was crouching there, watching them recede, when a large shadow made him scrunch even deeper.

A Demolition Crab was hovering over the observatory, one trembling winch at each corner. Archer banged his fake leg up the road to a cliff overlooking the new quarry. In the distance the Burghs loomed like Oz, stretching all across the horizon until the buildings were lost in smog. Archer looked back. The skin was wide open; a crew was dragging out an oversize body bag that left a slimy serpentine trail.

The boy flopped down and had a good long cry. When he was all wept-out he pushed himself back up and stood looking over the quarry. There wasn't a soul around. Archer pulled the jar from under his coat and carefully peeled up its soft cloth cover. Shading it with his body, he peeked left and right, then tentatively placed his lips on the rubbery black diaphragm. It had a funny chemical taste, so he pursed his lips and whispered quickly, *"Solo!"*

Immediately the jar filled with a swirling haze. Archer shrieked and tossed it like a hot potato. The glass broke on the rocky grade; the bottom half going one way, the top half the other, and a widening blurry pinwheel racing down between them. Archer whirled on his prosthetic leg and, screaming like a woman, ran *hwee hwee hwee* all the way home.

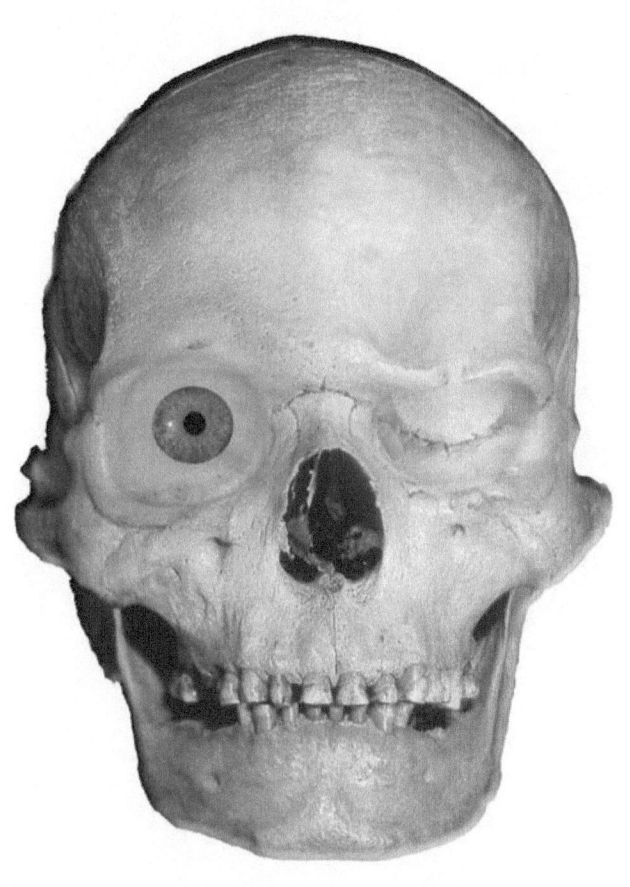

www.ingramcontent.com/pod-product-compliance
Lightning Source LLC
Chambersburg PA
CBHW051828170626
46807CB00003B/1075